Her Heart's Desire

A LETTING LOVE IN STORY
BOOK TWO

DAWN BACA

Dedication

To my devoted husband Jeremy,
you are my heart, my soul, my inspiration. Thank you
for lifting me up to reach the stars, and being there to
remind me you'll always catch me if I fall. Our
adventures are far more exciting together,
than they ever could be apart.

And to Aunt Vickie,
thank you for being my friend, my champion. Even
before you met me, you were by my side and I will be
forever grateful. The void you left behind has been a
wide chasm to bridge.
You are missed more than words.

My love for you is a journey starting at forever and ending at never.

—— Anonymous

It started with a kiss...

PROLOGUE

1988
Claude

Eight-year-old Claude Durand watched his best friend Sophie Compte scrunch up her nose as she squished the wiggling worm onto a hook before throwing her fishing line back into the water.

Sophie groaned. "Gak! Why do we have to use worms?"

"Why not?" He choked back his laughter. "Look, you hold it like this, not squishing it, and spear it on the hook." He showed her how his father had taught him.

"But they wiggle." She pursed her lips and twisted up her face again.

He rolled his eyes. *She's such a girl.* "They need to wiggle to bait the fish."

She nodded, clearly trying to follow his instructions.

He loved doing new stuff with her. Her father had taught them to ride horses, and his father was teaching them to fish. And though she hated the live worms she found the best ones for fishing under stones, directing him so he could scoop them into a glass jar.

He glanced at the flurry of scratches on her thin legs and arms, evidence of their adventures climbing trees. She would dare him to climb to the highest branches of the oak trees, and he would rise to the challenge by scooting up and not looking down. Sophie was the bravest person he knew. When his father told them ghost stories at night while camping, she never winced or cowered.

He loved their summer trips to *La Forge de Saint Marie* where their families camped together for the month before they had to return to school. The resort was nestled in a remote area of the Haute Marne, just outside of the Champagne region.

Her eyes twinkled. The little creases around them when she laughed made her prettier. His mother called them crows' feet and hated them, always putting creams on before bed to make them disappear. He didn't understand the point, and hoped when they got older Sophie would love the way they looked on her as much as he did.

"What are you thinking, Claude?" Sophie asked.

He shrugged. "That I'm going to marry you someday."

She rolled her eyes and laughed. "We're too young to be thinking of marriage."

"It's never too soon to think about your future."

"A lot can change before we grow up. You'll probably run off with some famous model and marry her."

He had no doubt he would marry her. He leaned over and pressed a kiss to her cheek.

"Claude, what are you doing?" She wiped her cheek with the back of her hand.

His father laughed behind them. "You need to ask permission, Claude, before you kiss a *mademoiselle*."

"But you don't ask *Maman* when you kiss her."

"Yes, but we are married, son."

"I'm going to marry Sophie someday."

"You had better ask her papa for her hand first," his father said.

Sophie grimaced. "I don't want to marry. We're only eight, Claude."

"Not now, silly," he said. He felt so much older than her. After all, his birthday was six months before hers. "One day," he said.

Sophie squealed just as her fishing pole started to vibrate in her hand. "Fish! It's a fish!" She bounced up and down, laughing.

Claude's father, Rémy, ran over and helped her reel it in. "Good job, young lady. That's an impressive trout. We'll eat like kings tonight."

The fish writhed and wiggled on the line until he unhooked it and put it in their bucket of water.

Sophie peered into the bucket as the fish swam around in circles. Claude stood beside her and looked down at the other fish they'd caught that morning. As she lifted her head, she bumped his nose.

"Ow!" Claude stumbled backward.

"Sorry!" she cried.

"Here, let me look." His father lifted his chin. "Ah, not broken." Rémy ruffled Claude's hair.

Claude nodded, and wiped away the tears gathering before they could fall. His nose smarted, but he'd never let Sophie know how much it hurt. She'd feel bad.

Setting their poles aside, they moved over to the blanket spread out on the grass under a large gnarled oak tree and sat down. Claude pulled out the bag of crisps and handed them to Sophie. The basket was filled with beet salad, carrots, grapes, apple slices, Camembert cheese, baguettes, and homemade brownies from Sophie's mom.

Under the shade of the tree, they relaxed and finished their lunch, calling out and pointing when the water rippled in the small lake as the fish jumped up and made little splashes on the surface. After lunch, they fished until the sun dipped in the sky.

"Okay, kids, let's head back before your mothers come to fetch us." Rémy gathered the poles and the heavy bucket full of fish.

Sophie helped Claude pack up the picnic basket, and as he was bent over he found a prize. He reached down, plucked a dandelion from the ground, and offered it to Sophie.

"Make a wish," Claude said.

Sophie closed her eyes, and with a soft whoosh of breath blew the white, featherlike seeds. She opened her eyes in time to see them float away on the breeze. With a smile she released the stem, and the three of them walked back to their campsite.

"Sophie, will you be joining us to watch the comet tonight?" Rémy asked.

Sophie nodded. "I wanna come and see. I'll check with *Maman* when we get back."

"Papa put the telescope behind our tent, over-looking the field. He showed me the big black sky all lit up with glittery stars last night as he set it up," Claude said.

"It helped that there was no moon, so the sky was more vibrant than usual," Rémy said.

"Sounds pretty," Sophie said.

"It was. In the telescope they look so close, almost as though you could reach out your hand and scoop them up," Claude said.

"Ahh," Sophie sighed, her eyes lifted to the sky, a wistful expression on her face.

Claude slipped his hand into Sophie's as they walked back, and she didn't pull away. His father winked at him when he caught his stare, causing a wide grin. It was probably splitting his face open enough to light the night sky itself.

This is the best day ever.

CHAPTER 1

Waking Up Alone

2006
Sophie

S ophie Compte rubbed her arms against the chill as she wandered out past Paddock A looking for her boyfriend, Claude. Her damp hair was pulled into a clip behind her head, the tendrils sticking to her cheeks. Frustration filled her as the cold air bit into her skin through a meager angora sweater. Due to her hasty departure, she'd left her jacket behind. She knew he'd come directly to the farm since his car was parked in front of his mother's house. A stable boy was loading hay bales onto a rolling cart when she walked past the barn.

"Good morning. Have you seen Claude today?"

"*Oui, Mademoiselle*, he's in the stables."

"*Merci*," Sophie said, twisting around and heading toward the back of the property, a determined step in her stride.

Her hands clenched, her head was down, conscious of where her feet landed, always careful of the uneven ground of the horse farm.

"*Bonjour*, Claude."

"Good morning, Sophie. Did you sleep well?" The twinkle in his deep blue eyes lacked the understanding she craved.

"Well enough, though I was lonely this morning." Sophie pouted.

"Darling, we've discussed this. I cannot stay with you in the mornings." Claude's eyes clouded as he looked over her shoulder.

"You are being ridiculous. Papa knows and approves."

Claude's brow furrowed slightly. "Maybe so, but I will not be caught cavorting with the boss's daughter in his own home. It isn't proper. I've come too far to ruin it now."

"And being with me would ruin it?" Sophie's voice had a thread of steel running through it.

Claude set down his clipboard and took her in his arms. She stiffened at his touch. He kissed her forehead before lifting her chin and looking her straight in the eye. "*Ma chérie*, you are my light. But you are the boss's daughter. I want to be seen for my own work, not for sleeping my way to the top."

Sophie relaxed slightly and wrapped her arms around his waist. "You're graduating with honors and are now a full-fledged large-animal veterinarian. You've done that all on your own."

"And I work for your father. And, in some respects, you as well."

"Fine. You're fired."

"Sophie," Claude growled.

"What?" She pushed against his chest, backing up a step and tossing her hands in the air. Her eyes narrowed, and her shoulders squared. "You won't marry me because you work for my family. So don't. Marry me instead."

"I can't."

"You stubborn fool. I won't wait forever. Remember that, *Monsieur* Durand." She stormed from the stables, her back stiff and her chin set. Her new waterproof boots squished in the soft dirt as she fled. The traitorous tears welling in her eyes were too much to bear.

The inflexible, insufferable fool.

"Sophie, wait," he called out.

She tuned him out. There was plenty of work to do today and she refused to let his pride aggravate her further, though her irritation grew with each step. They would be graduating vet school shortly, and she had long since thought that was what he was waiting for. He loved her. And not just for her family's money or connections.

Her mind wandering, Sophie walked right into the massive chest of the stable manager.

"*Mademoiselle*."

"*Pardon*, Eddie."

"You have a call."

"*Merci*, I'll take it in the office."

Eddie nodded and stepped aside. Sophie entered her office and shut the door behind her. Settled at her desk, she picked up the line next to the little red blinking light.

"*Bonjour*, this is Ms. Compte." The words came as a reflex when she was at the farm's office.

"Doctor, how are you?"

The voice on the other end was a welcome distraction.

"Addison, what a joy. You are a breath of fresh air." Sophie grinned at the ceiling. Slouching back in her chair, the tension eased from her shoulders as she pressed the handset closer to her ear.

"Things that bad, huh?"

Dodging the question, she asked, "Speaking of doctors, how's that husband of yours doing?" Sophie glanced at the framed photograph on her desk of her dear friend and her family.

"Sergei is fine. I'm calling to see what day would be best for us to come."

"Come? To Paris?"

"Uh, yeah." Addison paused. "...for your graduation. It's at the end of the month, right?"

"*Oui, pardon,* I'm distracted today." A quick glance at the large calendar on her wall with a thick red circle around a date at the bottom of the page confirmed this.

"I can tell. Talk to me, my friend."

"Oh, the usual. I honestly never thought I'd meet someone more stubborn than you."

"Thanks, I think." Addison laughed.

"*Pardon*, I'm *exaspéré*. I shouldn't take it out on you."

"We wanted to book our flights, and thought we'd stay over for a few extra days if that works for you."

"*Oui, mon amie,* time with you is always welcome. The children? My little Maxeem?" she said, drawing out a long *e* sound instead of the *i*. Her weekly Skype calls to see the children growing weren't the same as being able to squeeze them in person.

"Yes, Maxim and Natalya are coming. Although I think it's crazy to bring the munchkins with us."

"Good, and you will stay with us. Papa insists."

"He may regret it with two little ones running around his beautiful house. They're a handful."

"It will be good practice for him." Sophie sighed.

"Something I should know?" Addison asked.

"Of course not. I can't even get the stubborn man to stay in bed with me when the sun rises. I certainly can't get him to marry me."

Addison let out a hearty laugh. "Get him to marry you, wow, that sounds like a tough order."

"That headstrong mule. He's being ridiculous because he works here."

"Oh, no. Don't tell me you fired him."

"*Oui*, and he just laughed at me."

The cord from the phone knocked over the pencil cup on her desk, spilling the pens and pencils across her desk. With a groan, she slipped the scattered pencils and pens into the cup before tilting it back upright.

"Good, because that's not how you want him."

"*Non*. I know this. But damn it. He's so *compliqué*."

A loose pencil slid across the desk, landing in her lap. She threw it across the room. The sharp tip stuck to the wood-paneled wall briefly before dropping to the floor with a clatter.

"Patience, my friend. Patience. Your day will come."

"Come on Wednesday. And you can stay until the following week?" Sophie asked.

"Of course."

"*Magnifique*. We are looking forward to your visit. I will make all of the arrangements."

"Sophie, you don't need to do that."

Sophie shrugged. At the continued silence, she realized she hadn't said anything and that Addison couldn't see her. "What good is being filthy rich if you can't spoil those you love?"

"I love you, too, my friend. We'll see you soon."

"*Oui*. Be safe. Give the littles my love."

As Sophie dropped the phone back into its cradle, Bertrand Compte rapped on the frosted glass pane in the door and called out her name. Scowling, she looked up as her father's head popped in through the crack in the doorway. Her eyes narrowed at her cashmere coat draped over his arm.

"Sophie, are the records for Balthazar ready?"

"*Oui*, Papa. I'll need a few minutes to get them in

order." She looked down at the piles of paperwork littering her desk and huffed out a long breath.

"Great. Who was that?" He gestured at the phone on her desk.

"Addy. They are coming to the ceremony. I'd forgotten."

"*Magnifique*. And the children?"

Sophie laughed. "*Oui,* they are bringing the babies. Though she did give a warning that they were a handful."

"Good. Good." Bertrand waved his hand in dismissal. "What has you in such a sour mood?"

"Claude."

"Patience, my darling child. Give the man time."

She rolled her eyes. "You sound like Addison. She just said the same thing."

Bertrand chuckled. "He needs to feel like he's his own man. By the way, here's your coat. Agnes said you ran off this morning in a huff."

"How is this ever going to work if he stays?"

"The same way that it would work if he goes. All relationships require mutual affection and mutual respect. So stop trying to fire him."

Sophie's eyes grew wide as heat filled her cheeks. "How did you know?"

"Because he's moping around the stables like a fool in love."

"Oh, Papa." She propped her elbows on the desk and folded her hands under her chin.

"Stop pouting, my girl. Start plotting." Bertrand draped the coat over the hook on the wall behind the door.

She giggled. "That sounds positively devious."

"It should. Your mother's blood runs through those veins. I've never met anyone with the gift of matchmaking like you. So deal with it, and get back to work. *Monsieur* Martin will be here this afternoon for Balthazar and will expect everything in order."

"*Oui*, Papa. I'll have everything ready for you."

"It's a big day. Your first successful breeding is leaving the nest."

"I know." Sophie sighed.

"I'm so proud of you, Sophie. You've studied hard, you've a great head for the business, and your instincts for breeding are second to none. We've never been in better hands."

"Thanks, Papa." Sophie's lips curved as she met his gaze. Her heart swelled at his praise. Making him proud made all of her accomplishments brighter.

"Now, there's a good girl. I'll see you at lunch."

Sophie nodded as her father blew her a kiss and

closed the door with a click behind him, leaving her alone with her thoughts once again.

I won't run this time. Though she had no regrets about studying in Russia, because she'd met Addison and Sergei and wouldn't trade those friendships for anything, it hadn't changed things with Claude. She still loved him and still wanted to marry the obstinate jerk.

She didn't know how she'd knock sense into that man, but she would eventually figure something out. With a heavy sigh, she scooted her chair closer to the desk and opened the records she needed to print out for the horse's sale.

CHAPTER 2

Temptations

Claude

Claude Durand watched the love of his life walk away, her shoulders tight, her stride determined. *Damn it.* He'd be sleeping alone tonight. Ah, well, he owed his mother a dinner, so he'd make the best of it.

He picked up the clipboard and scanned the top sheet. Fighting with Sophie was taxing his last nerve. He couldn't focus on the notes in front of him.

He loved Sophie, but he couldn't deviate from his plans. Becoming a large-animal veterinarian was only the beginning. He needed to secure his position at the farm. Once he saved enough money to ensure his mother's future was taken care of, he could properly propose. The last seven years had been all about studying hard and saving every euro he could. He had a ring in mind but he was nowhere near ready yet. He couldn't ask Sophie's father for her hand under his present circumstances. It just wouldn't be right, the pauper asking for the hand of the princess.

Sophie didn't agree, she couldn't understand, and she figured things would always stay the same. He'd tried to explain. Her whole world was financially stable. She couldn't relate to the fact that he needed to save for his mother's future as well as his own.

"Hello, there." He soothed the anxious foal standing before him. The energy in the stables had everyone restless.

Especially him.

Today, Balthazar was leaving. Magnus's sire was such a beautiful, gentle soul, and everyone's favorite yearling by far. All the foals born on the farm were precious, though some seemed to wiggle their way further into his heart. Claude coaxed Magnus into eating another piece of apple before he patted his neck and left to say his goodbyes to Balthazar.

The yearling was set to become another racehorse in the Martins' team. He would be treated like a king in his new home. Even more spoiled than he was at the Compte farm.

She's so contrary. He kicked a pebble in the dirt. Why couldn't she see it was important he become something? To be more than just the boy whose father once ran her family's stables? They had been inseparable since they were children. Best friends. He'd never known anyone like her, so selfless and so giving, yet she could never understand the drive he had or the need to be more. It was not only for himself, but for her as well.

He'd studied to become a veterinarian to secure his future so he would always be needed and wanted at the farm, to be a worthy and equal partner to Sophie. Claude was only ten years old when his father died of a heart attack. Sophie's mother had stepped in and requested they remain on the farm, giving his mother a job as Marte's assistant and assuring them they would always be welcome and have a home there for as long as they wanted.

Just over a year after his father's death, Sophie's mother died. Bertrand and Sophie spent less and less time at the stables at first, and by the time things returned to normal a new fire had been lit within him. Then that Camilla woman came and sent Sophie away to boarding school. Gritting his teeth, he recalled how sure he'd been that they would be sent away as well.

Claude knew he would need to be strong, to work

hard and become indispensable. To be the best he could be, not only for his mother but for Bertrand and Sophie as well.

Slowly making his way to Balthazar's gate, he watched as the horse flicked his ears in greeting.

"Hey, boy, ready for your new home?"

Balthazar nuzzled his palm.

Claude rested his forehead against the horse. "*Oui,* I know you only love me for my treats."

Balthazar nodded against his forehead, banging it as he bobbed.

"See, I knew it."

The horse neighed. Laughing, Claude reached into his jacket pocket, pulled out apple slices, and held them out in his flat palm. The horse nibbled at the pieces as Claude rubbed his neck with his other hand.

"There you go, boy. Enjoy."

The horse made quick work of the apple slices.

"I'm going to miss you around here."

Balthazar whinnied.

Claude fed him another apple slice. Balthazar neighed as he bobbed his head again.

"Be a good boy now. I'll see you soon."

After patting the horse again, he stepped away from the stall. He strolled out to Paddock A to observe the trainers walking a couple of the fillies in circles, getting them used to halters.

He leaned against the railing, watching the graceful strides of the foals as they were led around. Being around the horses was soothing and relaxing. They were such gentle creatures.

"Chin up, son."

The voice behind him startled him out of his head. Sophie's father came up beside him and rested his hand on Claude's shoulder.

"Good morning, sir."

"Oh, don't give me that 'sir' nonsense. We're family, or will be one of these days."

Claude's eyes grew wide as his breath caught in his throat. "Sir?"

Bertrand gave him a side eye. "Oh, come now. We both know you're crazy stupid about my girl. And she loves you back."

Claude nodded.

"So, when you're ready, I'll be expecting a visit."

"I have your blessing?"

"When you're ready. Come to me and we'll talk," Bertrand said. He patted him on his shoulder, and with a wave to the men in the paddock he strode away.

Claude felt a huge weight land back on his shoulders as *Monsieur* Compte retreated. Having his approval, though not in so many words, was a blessing and a curse. He would have to step up his game, because there was no alternative now. Not only was Sophie anxious for his proposal, but clearly her father was expecting it as well.

Just what I needed.

CHAPTER 3

Au Revoir

Sophie

Sophie triple-checked the file for Balthazar. She needed to make sure a copy of the paperwork covering his medical history, the evaluation and approval from the French Ministry of Interiors' Racing and Gaming Department, his pedigree, as well as his training records, were included.

Satisfied it was complete, she closed the folder and slipped it into a large manila envelope, placing it neatly on the corner of her desk. This last task left her a bit melancholy. Resting her hand on the pile of paperwork, she took a deep breath. The breeding process producing Balthazar had been her first experience as a trained specialist. Balthazar was the first to leave the nest, and his departure left a hollowness. Checking the clock, she noted it was already a quarter to noon. Her father expected her for lunch today. With a sigh, she shut down the computer and pushed out of her chair. Thankful for the jacket, she slipped it on before leaving the office in the barn, closing the door behind her. She pulled her coat tight around her body to ward off the cool spring breeze as she headed to the main house. The chill in the air seemed to mirror her mood perfectly. The old house held a special place in her heart. It was where her family had been complete.

Climbing the steps, she laid a hand on the top of the handrail and took in her surroundings. The memories collided. Her mother's smiling face, the twinkle in her eyes when she looked at her father. The way her mother stroked her hair as she brushed it before putting her to bed with a lullaby. Sophie had been surrounded by happiness here. A cocoon of love. Her parents had loved each other deeply, and their love for her was always present.

Some mornings, the memories flooded in and wrapped themselves around her, making her feel like her mother was still with them. She stroked the worn wood of the banister. The farm would always be the last remaining tie to her mother.

Which was why the hag Papa had later married

demanded they move into an apartment in the city. Camilla was the polar opposite of her mother. But her father had been lonely and under her spell. So, Sophie was sent to boarding school, and Papa and Camilla moved into the apartment, which wasn't so bad— though she missed the fresh air of being on the farm, the smell of the hay, the horses. All the things Camilla hated. Ah, well, good riddance to bad rubbish. She was gone now, with her insufferable attitude and her extensive luggage collection. That brought a smile to Sophie's lips.

"*Bonjour, Mademoiselle.*"

Startled from her stroll down memory lane, Sophie hugged the house manager. "Marte, how are you this fine morning?" Sophie gave her another squeeze. The house manager was a small, slightly plump woman with a kind, wise face, in her early sixties and aging with dignity.

"*Très bien.* You are too skinny, child. Come, let me fatten you up."

Sophie laughed. "You've been saying that since I was a child."

"You still are a child to me. And you are still too skinny." Marte shook her head and clucked her tongue against her teeth. "Your father is in the dining room."

"Thanks. I need to wash up first," Sophie said as

she led the way to the kitchen. She could have used the powder room down the hall, but she preferred the bustling energy of the kitchen.

Halfway down the hall, the screen door opened and slapped closed. As she turned around, she caught a glimpse of Claude heading into the powder room.

Her shoulders slumped. She had hoped to avoid him the rest of the afternoon, but clearly that wasn't in the cards.

Marte patted her arm. "Ignore him, *ma chérie*; he is just a boy."

"Oh, Marte, I wish that was the case." She felt a pang in her chest.

Marte shook her head but said nothing more. They continued down the hall in silence. Greeting the cook, she kissed his cheek. "*Bonjour*, Carson. Something smells sinful."

Carson beamed as she headed for the large farm-house-style sink against the far wall. A master chef in his own right, Sophie's mother had wooed Carson away from a five-star hotel in Normandy when she was a little girl. Her father could never say no to any of her mother's whims. And Carson had been with the family ever since. She had no idea how old he was; he looked like he hadn't aged a day since he'd come. His dark hair still had no hint of grey, and his pale skin showed no sign of wrinkling. Only the corners of his eyes held creases, evidence of his quick wit and easy laughter. He knew her favorites by heart and made a point to always bake her something amazing when she spent the day at the farm.

After scrubbing her hands she grabbed a fresh date out of the bowl on the center island, then made her way to the dining room. Her father was already seated at the head of the wooden table, and Claude sat to his right. Looking at Bertrand, one would hardly guess he was a world-renowned horse breeder sitting at the table in his worn jeans and faded flannel.

Sophie took the spot her mother once used, on her father's left. Under the placemat at the seat to her left, faint scars from when she had drawn in the table still remained.

"Ah, Sophie, you are here. Carson has a treat for you," Bertrand said.

"*Oui,* Papa. That would be the blueberry cheesecake in the oven." Under her lashes, she caught Claude staring at her mouth as she licked her lips. Without acknowledging him, she turned her attention back to her father.

"Nothing gets past you." Bertrand chuckled.

"I stopped by the kitchen on the way in to give him my love, and I could smell it."

"Of course you did."

Lunch was a quiet affair, everyone subdued about the imminent departure of Balthazar. Bertrand and Claude discussed how the weaning of the horses was going. Her attention was distracted, so she wasn't following the conversation as closely as she usually would. She pushed the food around her plate, her appetite lost. The tension in the air between Claude and herself made the butterflies in her stomach riot. She hated when they argued.

After finishing her coffee and cheesecake, she excused herself with a kiss on her father's cheek. Once she paused to give a dismissive goodbye to Claude, she rushed back to her office.

Closing the door with a decisive click, a loud sigh escaped her as she rested her head against it. The phone rang, its sharp jangling reminding her the world didn't stop. She pushed away from the door. Life was calling, whether she was in the mood or not.

CHAPTER 4

Finding Faults

Claude

C laude walked into his house, his shoulders slumped. Sophie had ignored him for the most part, talking only to *Monsieur* Martin as they loaded up Balthazar and watched him leave. After kicking off his boots in the tiled entryway, he wiggled his now-free toes.

Following the voices, he found his mother in the kitchen having coffee with Jacques, the new horse trainer. "*Hallo,*" he said.

"Oh, Claude, *bonjour*, I was just leaving," stumbled Jacques. "Leila, thanks for the coffee." He ambled out the door, his slight limp appearing more pronounced than usual.

"No need to rush out on my account." Claude walked over to the counter and poured himself a cup of coffee as Jacques slipped out of the room. The screen door banged against the frame as he exited. That was odd. *What's his problem?*

"How was your day?" his mother asked, not meeting his eye.

He couldn't put his finger on it, but the hair on the back of his neck seemed to rise as he stared at his mother. "What was that about?"

"Ah, nothing. We're just friends." Leila shrugged dismissively.

"It's okay to be more than friends, too, *Maman*. I worry about you being lonely."

Leila smiled, though it didn't reach her eyes.

He sat down at the table and sipped his coffee.

"And how is Sophie?" she asked.

"Mad at me."

"What did you do this time?"

"Why do you always assume it's my fault, *Maman*? Why can't it be her fault for being so pig-headed?" he asked.

She laughed so hard there were tears in her eyes. "You are a man. It usually is the man's fault. That's how it works."

"That's pretty sexist."

This only made his mother laugh harder. "So, come now, tell me. Why is Sophie upset?"

"Because she wants to get married."

"And you no longer wish to marry her?" She cocked her head to the side and stared at him.

"Of course I do. I love her." He gripped the coffee cup a little harder.

Leila moved from her seat to the counter and filled her cup. "So, what's the problem?"

"Now's not the time." Claude gulped his coffee. "Ugh." He choked as the coffee burned its way down his throat.

"I wasn't aware there was a 'right' time when you are in love."

"It's not that simple. I have things to do first."

"Ah, like I said. Your fault."

"How is having a plan my fault for Sophie being mad at me?" he huffed.

"The entire purpose of marriage is a partnership with another person. A person you love and respect, and trust to stand by your side during hardships as well as the good times."

"*Oui*, I know that."

"And you still don't see why Sophie is upset? That is why it is usually the man's fault." She shrugged.

"How is wanting to be responsible before I get

married a bad thing?" he asked. "One would think it would be appreciated that I don't rush in."

"Son, you've known her most of your life. This could hardly be called rushing in."

"You know what I mean. I'm working as hard as I can to save money."

"So why not tell her this? You can offer her the future, and still wait to get married."

Claude choked on his coffee. "Sophie won't allow for a long engagement, and she'll plan a huge, elaborate wedding as fast as she can. So I only have one chance to get it right."

"Are you sure about that?" Leila asked.

"Oh, *Maman*, of all the things I question that is one I'm absolutely certain of. In order to do this, I need to be established first." He bit his lip as his gaze searched for understanding from his mother.

"Alas, my boy, there lies the problem. You want to do it before your partnership, not with your partner. That is why Sophie is hurt." She gave him a wide grin before lifting her cup. "Do you think your father and I waited until he was established before we wed? *Non*, of course not. Had we waited, we may not have had the chance to marry. Or to have you, for that matter."

Claude's head dropped to his chest. *Of course.*

Sophie wanted to be a part of it, and he was shutting her out.

"Time is a luxury not all of us have," she said softly.

"I just want to be worthy of her, *Maman*," he mumbled.

"She believes you already are." She rested her hand on his.

He lifted his head and frowned.

She stroked his cheek. "Let's have a nice dinner and forget our troubles for tonight."

"What troubles have you, *Maman*?"

"Nothing, just a figure of speech."

Claude paused, and seeing nothing in his mother's face to say otherwise he let it go. "I like that idea. I'll go wash up now," he said before hurrying down the hall to the bathroom.

After dinner his mother poured them each a glass of wine, and they walked out to the porch to enjoy the light breeze and to watch the colorful sky as the sun took its leave.

"*Maman*, why didn't you remarry after Papa died?" he asked.

"I've never desired to replace what I had with your

father. When he died, I guess a part of me was buried with him. I had you and the memories of what we shared, and somehow that was enough," Leila said.

"Don't you get lonely?"

"Son, if you are looking for more excuses to put Sophie off, it won't work. I had the love of my life. I had everything. I don't regret marrying young, though we were cautioned against it. We had a good life together." With a sigh his mother looked down her nose at him, as she had often enough throughout his childhood.

"I worry about you. I want to make sure you are secure."

"Claude, the Comptes have always made sure I was secure. You as well. You forget all they have done for us."

He shook his head. "*Non, Maman.* I have not. I just don't think we can expect it to last forever."

"And why is that? You will marry Sophie. Bertrand will retire. And I shall stay here at the farm, waiting for the grandbabies that will visit."

Claude flinched. "You sound like you've got this all figured out."

She sipped her wine and stared up at the sky, taking a deep breath before responding. "I think you may be the only one who hasn't yet."

"You are supposed to be on my side, *Maman*," he grumbled.

Taking a sip of wine, he turned his gaze up to the blazing fire that scattered across the slowly-darkening sky. The sky reminded him of his father. Claude's father had loved to sit under a black sky dotted with a smattering of glowing pinpricks of light and point out the constellations and clusters of stars to him. Sometimes they even peered at the sky through a telescope, bringing the stars to life, up close and personal. Nothing had been the same since his father died.

"I am on your side. I will support you regardless. However, that said, I think Sophie is a wonderful girl and the perfect partner for you. I hope you don't jeopardize that by being inflexible."

Claude shook his head. His mother wasn't easing his frustration. In fact, he was just more annoyed that everyone seemed incapable of seeing his reasoning. He needed to talk to Sophie.

CHAPTER 5

Absence of the Heart

Claude

Claude stared at the ceiling of his bedroom, trying to get his bearings. He had not slept well. He usually didn't when Sophie wasn't by his side. Though he would never admit it, he understood why she hated waking up to find him gone in the mornings. It was the same emptiness he felt now, lying in his bed alone, wishing she was beside him.

With a heavy sigh, he tossed the blankets off and climbed out of bed. He would have breakfast with his mother before he started the day. He missed Sophie terribly. Hated the distance between them. Every day she didn't talk to him led to the possibility of a longer separation. He could only hope this wouldn't lead to another one of their long breakups like in the past. Reaching for his phone, he saw that the screen showed no messages. For a brief moment he considered texting her, but knew there was no point. She wouldn't talk until she was ready.

Dressing quickly, he pulled the covers over his bed and tucked the ends in. No matter how hard he tried, he could never make his bed look as perfect as his mother did with little effort. After picking up the clothes strewn around the floor, he tossed them into the hamper and straightened up his room. If he didn't his mother would, and he hated being an additional burden to her.

The house was quiet. Too quiet. He'd expected to hear his mother bustling about in the kitchen but, walking down the hall, he discovered that the room was dark and his mother was absent.

A note on the counter propped up by a fresh pot of coffee had his name scrawled across it. His mother's familiar penmanship greeted him.

At the main house today.
All hands needed to scrub for the party.
See you for lunch?

"So much for breakfast," he sighed. After pouring a cup of coffee, he sat down at the table. There were fresh muffins in the basket, and he helped himself to one.

He would also be busy today, preparing the property for the party. He shook his head. To him, having such an ostentatious party simply because they had become veterinarians seemed a bit much. Even knowing it was futile, he tried to talk Sophie out of it. However, Bertrand insisted and his mother hounded him until he acquiesced and gave suggestions for the guest list.

A long sigh escaped him. His mother was thrilled and, in the end, that was what mattered most. His portion of the guest list was minuscule, to say the least, though the numbers would have mattered little in the scheme of things. Friends, family, and business associates of the Compte farm were all invited. Even the entire staff and their families had been included. The one thing he could say about the Comptes was that they were generous. Overly so.

This party was another example of the Comptes' penchant for over-the-top celebrations and an indication of what Sophie's and his wedding would be like. Bertrand had spared no expense. And it made Claude uncomfortable to see such extravagance where he was concerned. It brought back the feeling of being under a microscope, like when Bertrand had thrown a similarly elaborate party when they'd finished secondary school. He cringed, knowing this was what his future would be like. One of the reasons he found himself in no hurry. As a simple man of simple means, he had never been big on parties where he was the center of attention. For Sophie it was all she knew, and she thrived in the spotlight.

It didn't matter. This wasn't the first lavish party the Comptes had hosted, and it wouldn't be the last. He was just feeling self-conscious about being directly involved in the celebration. Then again, if he married Sophie he would need to get a grip because this would become a regular part of his life.

When. Not if... he chided himself.

They would marry, as long as he planned for it sooner rather than later. He struggled with the contradictions that battled within him. Though he didn't want to lose her, he wasn't ready to be her husband and all the position entailed either.

After downing the last of the coffee, he washed his cup and set the mug on the dripping tray. He then wiped down the table and counters and nodded. His mother didn't leave much for him to do around the house, so he took care to do the little things he could.

Claude slipped into his boots and headed to the stables. The party planners were coming today to begin the preparation for the area where the installation of the massive tents would take place, and to smooth the road out to prepare for the hundreds of cars that would come. It was Claude's responsibility to make sure the contractors had everything they needed while they worked.

If he wanted to check on the weaned ponies this morning, he needed to do it before everyone arrived and the work started. Seeing the horses grow was his greatest joy. The love of large animals also came from his father. And being near them, watching them thrive, made him feel closer to him. Even if only for a few moments on some days, he enjoyed his time with them. There had never been a doubt that this was where he belonged. Here with Sophie, the horses, and the fondest memories of his father.

CHAPTER 6

Retail Therapy

Sophie

Sophie opened her eyes in the dark room. She stretched her hand out, reaching for Claude, only to find the other side of the bed empty. Slapping the sheets, she rolled onto her back and closed her eyes, remembering their fight yesterday. It made her heart ache. She hated the emptiness inside when they were apart. Whether physically or emotionally, the gap always felt like a massive void in her soul.

Men. Why must they be so complicated? Oh, wait—

A shiver slid through her. Hadn't he accused her of the same often enough? Comparing her to Camilla. Giving her a hard time over things like her four sets of luggage, a different color for every season, and compression packing cubes to match.

With a heavy sigh, she opened her eyes again. Her body ached, as it often did when she'd had a restless night. The nightmares had come again. They only invaded her sleep when she was stressed or upset. Flipping the covers back, she got out of bed. When she yanked open the heavy damask drapes light flooded her room, causing her to squint and blink rapidly. She wasn't going to the farm today, so she wouldn't even be able to sneak glances at him, though she still was annoyed enough to not want to actually talk to him.

The housekeeper rapped on the door. After slipping into the room with a tray of coffee and croissants, she set it on the dressing table.

"Coffee, *Mademoiselle*."

"*Merci*, Agnes."

After showering, Sophie downed her cup of coffee and a warm buttered croissant as she dressed. Setting out in a rush, she was off to run some errands downtown.

"*Bonjour*, Hugo," Sophie said as their driver held the car door open for her.

"*Bonjour*, Ms. Sophie. Where are we headed today?" he asked.

"Drop me off at Studio 45, and if you could pick

me up this afternoon after lunch at *Les Jamais Après*, *s'il vous plaît*, I would appreciate it."

"*Oui, Mademoiselle.*"

Hugo drove her downtown in his usual efficient fashion. Having been a professional racecar driver in his youth, he was a master at zipping through traffic smoothly. When she was a child, he often told her stories on their drives. Twenty minutes later, he dropped her off at the day spa.

Sophie desperately needed a morning spent at the spa; it had been months since she had been properly spoiled and it showed. She had reserved the full Sanctuary package, an in-depth pampering, which included their signature facial and their classic mani/pedi, followed by a deep- tissue massage.

Four hours later, she stepped out of the spa just as uptight as she was when she crawled out of bed. She should have felt like a sparkling diamond. Instead, the tension hadn't left her neck and shoulders, and even the massage had done little to relax her.

Determined to put Claude out of her mind for the day she wandered down the cobblestone walkways, her lip between her teeth. Her frustration with him remained, and the day off her father had suggested wasn't working to ease any of the building irritation. It took every ounce of her energy to not be snippy with

Agnes and Hugo this morning. They didn't deserve her wrath because Claude made her pissy. Again. She stopped at Bistro Vendôme for a quick bite to eat. While she sat at the table at the little sidewalk café, an incredibly handsome waiter caught her attention.

"What is the pleasure of *mademoiselle?*"

"*Poulet au gratin et Café au lait.*"

The waiter scribbled her order into his notebook before filling her water glass with sparkling water and leaving.

Pulling out her new smartphone, a treat from her father for finishing veterinary school in the top three of her class, she tapped on the e-mail app and began scrolling through her messages. When lunch arrived ten minutes later, she picked at the chicken and potatoes on her plate while reading her emails. Nothing in her inbox was urgent. It was her futile attempt at trying to distract her mind from returning to Claude.

Pushing her plate aside she gave up on lunch, finished her coffee, and left cash on the table before returning to her errands.

Her plan was now to burn off the calories and disappointment with some serious shopping. She would buy a new dress for their ceremony and celebration, which, of course, required new shoes. If this didn't put her in a better mood, nothing would.

With a sigh, she stepped into the little boutique that always knew just what she needed. Tasha, the willowy blonde manager of the store, was there immediately with a tray of Champagne and chocolate-covered strawberries.

Ah, now we're talking.

"Bonjour, Mademoiselle," Tasha said.

Seated on the plush leather couch, Sophie sipped Champagne and waited for the parade of the latest styles to be brought out for her to view.

"Ms. Sophie, what brings you in today?"

"I need some cheering up."

"Ah. So, a little of everything." Tasha winked as she headed into the back room.

Within minutes the team of personal assistants came out, pulling three large rolling clothing racks from the back. Filled with bright colors, soft prints, and knee-length dresses, the racks were pushed to the center of the room.

The women pulled garments from the racks and displayed them with a flourish. With a nod or a shake of the head from Sophie, the items were moved around and set aside, depending on if she was considering trying them on, or not interested at all. At last, she was in her element.

Suddenly, the bustle of the room faded away, and

Sophie found herself tuned in to a hint of bronze silk tucked into the middle of the rack. She was usually a connoisseur of the little black dress, but there was something about this metallic silk fabric that pulled her out of her despondent mood.

Sophie stood and walked over to the rack, determined to ferret out the bronze calling to her. "May I?" she asked.

"*Oui.* Stunning, isn't it?" Tasha asked as Sophie pulled the shimmering dress off the rack and held it up to admire.

With a grin, she yanked open the door to the dressing room with a little more power than she'd anticipated and yelped as it slapped the wall with a loud thud. Finally, her mood was taking a turn. After rushing inside and pulling the door closed behind her, she unzipped the side of the sheath dress she wore and let it drop to the floor. She stepped into the silky bronze piece and slid it up her body. She smoothed her hands over her taut stomach and tugged it into place past her narrow hips before pushing open the door with her back facing out, so Tasha could zip up the dress.

Once in the middle of the room, surrounded by floor-to-ceiling mirrors, she pirouetted to gaze at the dress in every direction. The soft fabric brushed against her sun-kissed skin as she stared at her reflection in the mirror. It was magical. The sequins and small clear beads thick at the neck thinned and spaced out as they tapered off to the hem just above the knee. It glinted in the light as the fit and flare silk skirt glided like liquid gold against her thighs. The high neckline with capped sleeves covered every inch of her full breasts while accentuating them at the same time. Turning again, she smiled as the back tapered to a 'V', ending well above her natural waist, showing an appropriate amount of bare flesh.

"*Magnifique!* You make that dress shine," Tasha said, her fingers to her lips as she made a kissy sound.

Sophie slipped her feet into the nude-colored mesh and rhinestone pumps set before her. The signature red sole of the Louboutins peeked at her from the bottoms as she turned and modeled them, admiring her fresh pedicure through the open toe.

This is it. Sophie bobbed her head as she continued to stare at her image in the full-length mirrors. This was the dress she needed to turn Claude's head. And there it was. As hard as she tried to push him from her mind, he crept into her thoughts nonetheless.

CHAPTER 7

Temporary Truces

Claude

Claude slipped into the barn office and closed the door with a soft click. The radio on the desk filled the room with music.

Intent on the file she was reading, Sophie still hadn't looked up.

Slowly making his way over to the desk, careful not to scare her, he clutched the forget-me-nots he'd snagged from the back garden behind the house. If he did some stupid thing to hurt her feelings, the small purple flowers never failed to bring a smile to her lips. He'd often done or said careless things when they were children, so he was well-versed in mending fences with flowers.

He cleared his throat.

"When did you get here?" she gasped, her attention diverted from the file spread out before her.

He stood to the side of her now, peering down as the breath caught in his throat. Her hair slid over her shoulder. His hand itched to reach out and pull her hair back. God, he'd missed her.

Her brow was furrowed as though she was perturbed, but it couldn't still be about their fight. It had been almost a week since their argument. He'd left her alone to give her space. He hated when she was angry with him.

He thrust the flowers at her.

She narrowed her eyes. "We aren't children. Flowers can't fix everything anymore."

"Oh, come now. They're your favorites." He pressed them toward her.

And there it is.

A faint smile tugged at her lips as she took them from him and brought them to her nose. Closing her eyes, she inhaled the scent and her face lit up. When she opened her eyes, they were sparkling. The smile she'd first been so unwilling to part with split her face wide open.

"Am I forgiven?" he asked.

"*Non.*"

"Sophie," he growled. "Can we go for a walk before lunch? I've missed you."

Her response was a nonchalant shrug. After dropping the flowers into her half-filled water glass sitting by her monitor, she swiped the folder from the top of the file cabinet and flipped it closed then slid it back into the drawer before she locked the cabinet. His brow arched as she slipped the keys into her pocket and led the way out.

"When did you start locking your cabinets?" he asked.

"Hmm. Oh, just started."

His eyes narrowed but he let the matter drop for now. Once they were on the path toward the front of the farm, he stopped to pick a dandelion from the side of the road and extended it to her.

"Aren't we trying to save the bees?" Sophie asked.

"*Oui,* but one little flower from the side of the driveway won't change all the hard work Marte has put into the back garden and flowerbed. Besides, the bees and butterflies are already done with this one."

"She'll tan your hide one of these days if she figures out you're the one stealing her forget-me-nots."

Claude laughed. "Those are mine to pick as I choose."

"Oh, really? And how is that?"

"Because I asked Marte to help me find them when we were twelve."

Sophie's eyes grew wide.

"I told her they were to apologize to you. After the new stables were built and she planted the garden, the first thing she planted was a mess of forget-me-nots in the front corner so I wouldn't go traipsing all over the rest of the plants to get to them. She said she knew I would need them often."

Sophie laughed. "I never knew that."

"Marte is a romantic at heart."

"That she is." Sophie took the dandelion and raised it to her lips. Closing her eyes, she blew the tender white seeds into the wind.

"Did you make a wish?" Claude asked.

"*Oui.*"

"Then it will come true."

"I don't know about that."

"Patience, *ma chérie*. We are young still."

Sophie rolled her eyes at him. "I've waited more than fifteen years for you."

"That's not fair. You can't count back to when we were children."

"Sure I can. I've always known. You've had my heart from the beginning."

Claude leaned over and kissed her cheek. "And you have mine. Just be patient with me a bit longer."

Sophie pointed at him. "Besides, you told me you were going to marry me when we were eight."

He chuckled. "And if I recall, you told me you didn't want to get married."

Sophie scrunched her nose in response.

"So, what had you frowning when I came in?"

"You." She batted her eyelashes at him.

He grinned. "Besides me, what has you so serious? What's in that file?"

"I don't know." She pursed her lips.

"Come on, you can talk to me."

Sophie shook her head. "*Non.* Really. I don't know. I can't put my finger on it, but something feels off with our accounts."

"What file was it?"

"Just general expenses, petty cash, that kind of thing."

"*Le bien.*" Claude stuffed his hands in his pockets.

"But we seem to be spending more in the last three months than we have in the last two years."

"Now that's a big difference. What is the money being used on?"

Sophie patted the file. "That's just it—it looks legit. A couple of new vendors, a new leather supplier for bridles, harnesses, bits. An order for extra hay, the usual, I guess. But there are no notes explaining the changes like there usually is."

"Trust your gut. No one has better instincts than you."

"*Merci*," she said.

"With the breeding season behind us, there will be more time to dig into the business end of the stables."

"True."

"Any luck finding a replacement for farm manager?" he asked.

"*Non*. For now, I'll handle this while you handle the horses. Papa is still running everything else."

Claude bobbed his head. "Let's get away for the weekend. Visit the countryside for a few days to take our minds off of everything."

She gave him a sidelong glance.

"Come on, Sophie. We need some time alone."

"I'll think about it," she said as they headed to the house.

Even if he wasn't ready to marry her, she needed to know he still loved her and that their connection remained strong. Doubting him was only putting more distance between them.

CHAPTER 8

Fontainebleau

Claude

Claude peered over the newspaper he was reading to grin at Sophie. It had taken days to convince her to come away with him. They needed time. He needed more time.

The little hideaway was one of their constants. Just outside of Paris, the rented villa was nestled near the Fontainebleau forests and Barbizon, a charming little artists colony. Determined to enjoy the weekend since it would be their last chance to get away for some time to come, it was just what they needed to recharge after their final exams and the end of their last term.

This was his favorite part of the day, breakfast at the small table on the patio just outside the kitchen.

The pool sparkled, and the birds pecked away at the numerous feeders dotting the boundary of the yard. A soft breeze carried the aroma of blooming flowers and freshly cut lawn, adding to the serene ambiance.

Sophie held a steaming cup of coffee in her hand as she gazed at the sun peeking over the horizon.

Claude smirked as she leaned back in the chair and sighed. He loved seeing her relaxed. When they were alone, nothing else mattered. He wished the world would stop spinning sometimes so there could be more moments like this. Here, he could forget about all the obstacles in their path to a happy life together and pretend they were equals. No business worries, no concerns about working for her family. No reminders of the trappings of her wealth. Leaning over, he tugged a strand of her hair like when they were kids. Smiling, she reached out and caressed his cheek. When she looked at him like that, her eyes bewitching him, he was lost.

"How about lunch at *Le Cadran*, then shopping in the village?" Claude asked.

Sophie beamed. "I'll go take a shower now."

"Want help washing your back?"

"*Non.* I'll never get out of the shower then." She giggled.

Claude's brow rose.

She skirted away, leaving him on the terrace. While she might accuse him of distracting her in the shower, she needed no help taking forever when it came to getting ready for an outing. He would be here, waiting for at least another two hours. With a sigh, he returned his attention to the newspaper, flipping the pages of the sports section, and finished his coffee.

Two hours to the minute Sophie emerged from the house, primped and primed and as pretty as a princess, smelling of citrus and wildflowers.

"Your turn, though there might not be much hot water left," she said, kissing the top of his head.

"*Merci bien.* You should have let me shower with you—we could have saved water. Especially the hot water." Claude stood and swatted her behind with the folded newspaper.

Sophie rolled her eyes. "Oh, who are you kidding? Go now and get ready, I'm hungry."

"You just ate."

She waved her hand in dismissal. "A light snack two hours ago. I can't help having a fast metabolism."

Claude chuckled. He'd better make haste. Sophie was cranky when hungry, and that was a bear best left unpoked. Grinning, he made his way to the shower. Already accustomed to short, cold showers, this morning's ritual was nothing new.

Twenty minutes later, he joined Sophie in the kitchen. Standing off to the side, he watched her as she put away the dishes from the dishwasher. He loved watching her be domestic, not that he'd dare ever say that aloud.

"Ready?" he asked.

"*Oui,* just tidying up."

"How does a walk through the woods sound this afternoon?"

"*Tres bien.* Tomorrow, I'd like to visit the gardens at Château de Fontainebleau."

"Again? We've seen them before."

Sophie shrugged. "Only the English Garden. The Garden of Diana was closed the last two times, remember?"

"*Oui,* fair enough. But I have plans for us in the morning, so we'll do the gardens in the late afternoon, okay?"

Sophie nodded. Her eyes danced with mischief. "A surprise. Oh goody, what is it?"

"Later."

"*Non.* Now. I don't want to wait. Tell me now." Sophie rocked on her heels. "*S'il vous plaît.*"

Claude laughed, his breath coming out in a whoosh. She hated secrets and not knowing. Even wrapped gifts were never left in peace for long. Notorious for shaking and rattling them around, Sophie either guessed the contents or forced one to give in to protect the gift from breaking. In some ways, her enthusiasm was worse than a child's. "You are incorrigible."

"*Oui,* you know this about me." Sophie wrapped her arms around his neck, batting her eyelashes.

He was like putty in her hands. Turning his head away from her, he closed his eyes. He'd relent, he always did, but damned if he wasn't going to make her work for it just a bit.

"Pretty please," she whined.

He shook his head. "*Non,* you must learn to wait for your gifts." He snuck a glance at her from under his lowered lashes and stifled a grin as she frowned at him.

"I'm not a patient person."

"Don't I know it." Laughing, he wrapped his arms around her waist and pressed his cheek to her forehead. "Fine, but only if you're properly appreciative of the effort I've put into this."

"Always," she tittered.

With an exaggerated sigh, he said, "You really can't wait?"

"*Non,* tell me."

"Tomorrow morning at sunrise I've reserved a hot air balloon ride over the valley from the château." His chest filled with love as her eyes widened and her face split with the biggest smile.

She squealed, and bounced in place. "Fabulous! It's so romantic. I can't wait. I love you."

"And I, you. Though I really should have made you wait."

"*Non*. This way I can get up extra early to get ready so that we aren't late."

"True enough." He kissed her nose.

She pressed her lips to his before pulling away to grab her purse off the counter. "I'm really hungry now."

He chuckled. "Let's feed you before you turn into a monster, then."

The drive into town was peaceful with the windows down, letting the fresh air awaken their senses. Being early spring, tourist season wasn't in full bloom yet, so the roads were clear and the sidewalks uncrowded. This was the perfect time of year to visit.

The pub was almost empty when they entered. Only a handful of other people were seated at tables around the room. The low hum of voices in the background mixed with the soft music playing as Claude and Sophie sat at a table against the wide front windows overlooking the street.

They sampled the various suggestions the waiter

offered up, they shared a bottle of Chablis while people-watching. Fed, and no longer on the verge of hunger-induced violence, they enjoyed the art galleries and craft stores in the village square.

The bleating siren of the alarm went off at the ungodly hour of three o'clock in the morning. Claude groaned. He slapped the snooze button out of habit and rolled back over to snuggle with Sophie. She stroked his cheek before sliding out of bed.

"Where are you going?" he mumbled, opening an eye to peer at her.

"I've got to get ready. I have a date this morning to watch the sunrise." She yanked the covers back over her side of the bed, cocooning him under the warmth.

He closed his eyes again and tried to go back to sleep as Sophie flipped the water on. Her humming echoed in the bedroom. With another groan, Claude rolled onto his back and stared at the ceiling. It was pointless to hope he'd be able to go back to sleep, so he climbed out of bed and stripped off his boxer shorts before joining Sophie in the shower.

"Mind if I join you?"

Sophie groaned. "Are you afraid I'm going to use all the hot water?"

"Actually, I figured if I took a shower now I would be out of your hair while you get ready. And I can make coffee and heat up the croissants."

"Ah, you speak my language; bless you." She leaned in and gave him a light kiss before backing out of the way so that he could stand under the spray.

He made quick work of lathering up and rinsing. He leaned in, kissing the side of her neck, caressing it with his tongue and nipping at the wet skin.

She swatted at his chest. "Shoo now. I have to finish."

Cupping Sophie's face, he gave her a quick peck on the lips and stepped back out of the shower. He had taken less than ten minutes. He slid on jeans and a polo over his still-damp back before he padded down the hall to the kitchen to forage.

After a quick search of every cupboard, he found the bag of Sophie's favorite gourmet beans and prepared the coffee. With the croissants in the toaster oven, he tidied the kitchen. Inhaling, he filled his lungs with the deep nutty aroma of the beverage of the gods. It was the only thing that had half a chance of making Sophie human in the mornings. Restless, he pulled the carafe away from the dripping coffee. He filled two large mugs and carried them back into the bedroom.

Sophie stood at the sink in a pale-blue silk robe, her hair twisted up in a towel. She was humming again, as she did often when getting ready in the morning. He never tired of hearing her. There was something soothing about listening to her hum the popular children's lullaby, '*Au Clair de la Lune*'.

Leaving his cup on the dresser, he came up behind her and wrapped an arm around her, brushing his lips lightly across the back of her neck, and breathed in her perfume. A soft wave of ginger, bergamot, and citrus filled the air around her.

"Knock that off or I won't be ready in time," she said, giving his arm a slight pat as he laughed.

"Okay, the clock is ticking. Drink your coffee and hurry." He set her cup on the vanity and pressed a gentle kiss behind her ear, grinning as she trembled, before backing up. He tidied the room and headed back to the kitchen again with his own cup.

Drinking his coffee at the counter, he glanced at the clock on the wall as Sophie walked into the kitchen. He'd figured he had at least another forty minutes to wait for her to finish getting dressed.

"Surprised?" she asked.

"*Oui*, you're really early."

"I braided my hair, so I didn't have to dry and curl it." She laughed, giving a little spin.

"You look beautiful, as always." She took his breath away.

Standing, he grabbed the travel mugs and followed her out to the car. Stars still filled the black sky and the air held a slight chill. Their time away together was precious to him. Away from the predestined positions they both played at the farm or his concerns about not measuring up. Alone with her, the real world faded away.

When they arrived at the castle several massive balloons were already inflated, filling the area with bright colors. They made their way to the young man holding a clipboard, directing people to their locations. An adventurous spirit, Sophie was completely at ease with the small group surrounding the basket they were going up in, and within minutes they were fast friends.

Watching her in action was always inspiring. When she was dealing with strangers or business associates, she was intuitive and knew exactly what to say to people. She was genuinely interested in their stories, and they were comfortable sharing them. It was only him she lacked patience with.

Twenty minutes later everyone climbed into the oversized wicker baskets, and they were making their way airborne. The sensation of floating filled his stomach, and he had a brief sense of vertigo. The chill sharpened as they moved higher into the air. Purple-hued clouds pranced across the fire-filled orange and red sky as the sun began its ascent over the horizon. The beauty of the sunrise held him captivated as he tightened his embrace around Sophie. An almost deafening silence enveloped them, broken up by the occasional blast of the gas burner.

The grounds were highlighted in magnificent detail as they passed over the castle. The large moat sparkled under the growing light, as did the small lake behind it. Enormous sculptured fountains within the lake shot streams of water into the air before it trickled into the water below, dancing in ripples on the surface. Bright green grass was dotted with rows of perfectly shaped conical bushes aiming for the sky.

By the time they reached the Fontainebleau forests, they were so far up that it looked more like a poorly manicured lawn than a forest of individual trees. Sophie leaned in closer and kissed Claude under the chin. He leaned down and pressed his lips to hers, her lips curving into a smile under his.

On an exhale, his breath formed wispy puffs of air over Sophie's head. Snuggled up against him, looking out from their side of the basket, her laughter floated around them, making his heart swell with pride. Having her love was everything. It was moments like this, with his arms wrapped around her warm body, he started to question whether his reluctance to marry her was rational or just his insecurities manifesting into an excuse to delay what his heart already knew.

CHAPTER 9

Falling Deeper

Sophie

Sophie was over the moon as they walked hand-in-hand through the gardens of the castle. She loved flowers and plants and the calming effect their aroma had. Her mother had been a lover of all things green, and she'd had the thumb to prove it.

While she hadn't inherited her mother's green thumb, she possessed the same love and appreciation of all blooms and the sense of peace they brought. Being in the lavish gardens was like having her mother's warm embrace around her. She missed her most when strolling through places they would have shared a passion for. However, she was grateful she could share this with the love of her life.

The fountain of Diana, the Roman goddess of the hunt, stood regally, surrounded by large hunting hounds. Nestled in the center of the gardens, the statue and fountain were unique additions to the English-style gardens. This was a replica of course, as the original was safely tucked away at The Louvre. Walking along the edge of the pathway, she peered down the steps into the small pond surrounding the statue. One had to admire Henri II for his devotion to his mistress, even if it was flaunted in the face of his wife. There was no accounting for the stirrings of the heart. *Am I destined to want what I can't have? To love someone who will never fully be mine?* Holding Claude's hand, these musings tore into her previously-peaceful thoughts.

The wind whipped the spray of the fountain into the air, leaving her and Claude damp from the fine mist. The afternoon sped by as they wandered through the gardens, the vibrant colors of spring everywhere the eye could see.

"Have you seen enough, *ma chérie*?" he asked.

"*Oui*, I'm *affamé*, and could use a nap."

"*Très bien,* your wish is my command."

Exhausted once she was in the car, she rested her head against the window and was lulled to sleep by the movement. She awoke as they pulled up in front of the rented house.

"Would you like me to make lunch?" Claude asked.

"*Non,* just some nibbles, if you don't mind. I think I'm too tired to eat a proper meal."

"Of course. Go change, and I'll hunt something up for us. We can eat and then rest."

"*Merci.*"

Sophie felt like an entirely new woman after she'd washed her face and combed out her braid. Claude came into the bedroom a few minutes later with a tray of cheeses and sliced apples.

"*Magnifique.*"

Dropping into one of the overstuffed chairs next to the large double doors facing the fountain in the back garden she demolished the plate of goodies, her hunger sated momentarily.

Sophie stifled a yawn. Claude chuckled.

"You'll end up with your face in the plate if you aren't careful."

With a nod, she left the comfort of the chair and slid into bed. Once Claude joined her, she rested her cheek on his chest and traced her finger across his muscular abs. His heart drummed in her ear, the steady beat relaxing her. Closing her eyes, she drifted off to sleep.

Sophie sat at the edge of the hot tub, legs dangling in the water, sipping wine. The trees swayed in the soft breeze, and the sky filled with overlapping colors of red and orange as the sun lowered toward the horizon. The nap earlier had revived her energy. She wasn't a morning person, and they had been on the go since before dawn.

"More wine?" Claude held up the bottle of white wine.

"*Oui.*"

The Sauvignon Blanc was refreshing and crisp. The fruity flavors danced on her tongue, waking her taste buds.

They were back on the same page. Then again, as long as she didn't mention the future or children or marriage, they usually were. It was only when she pushed him on a topic he didn't want to pursue that their relationship went pear-shaped. She didn't understand him sometimes. *Truly, the most difficult man ever.* When they were children he talked about marrying her as though it was fated, like the future was set in stone. Yet now that they were of age, he shied away from those talks and plans more than ever.

Pushing those thoughts away she slid onto a seat

under the warm bubbling water, letting it caress her shoulders and neck. Claude leaned over, dipped his hand into the frothy liquid, and sprinkled the water at her.

"Hey," she squeaked.

Claude dropped into place beside her. The water sloshed around them as his body situated itself. The warm water soothed her muscles. Sitting there as the sun dipped further into its quest for slumber and the colors in the sky deepened, she was content.

The night creatures began to make their presence heard. Crickets chirped and owls hooted. It reminded her of the camping trips they went on as children and her early years of living on the farm. The sounds of nature soothed one's soul, instead of the bustling sounds of a city that never slept.

She set her glass on the tray behind them and slid over the narrow ledge between the hot tub into the adjoining pool. The sudden drop in temperature shocked her system. An involuntary shiver coursed through her body and goose pimples rose along her arms. Fully awake, she sank all the way under the water and swam just under the surface. The momentum of the water changed as Claude joined her.

Swimming underneath her, he wrapped his arms around her and then pulled them to the surface entwined. Laughing as their heads broke through, he leaned in and kissed her. Water streamed off her head, mingling with their kiss. Her tongue rolled over the salt coating her lips. The salt-water therapeutic pool was an added bonus to renting this villa.

She wrapped her arms around his neck and brought their bodies closer, the water flowing around them in a rush as the space between them shrank. He guided them to the shallow end where her toes skimmed the bottom with little effort.

As he dipped his head his lips grazed her neck just below the ear, making the heat rise within her and her heart skip a beat. Her breath caught in her throat as he placed featherlike kisses down her neck and across her collarbone. Her body quivered under his touch and her head tilted back as his kisses set her on fire.

He captured her lips with his, leaving her breathless. Her heart raced as she pushed up against the bottom with her toes and wrapped her legs around his waist, returning his passion with enthusiasm.

Claude moved them against the force of the water, holding her ass cheeks as he inched them closer to the side of the pool. Pushing her back up against the wall, he deepened the kiss. Her pulse raced as his tongue battled with hers, giving and taking with each pass inside her mouth. All thoughts escaped her as he tugged at the bow at the back of her neck. Her top slid down her breasts in slow motion as the knot gave way and the string loosened its hold.

He dropped his head to the hollow between her breasts, kissing her breastbone before sliding over and sucking a nipple between his teeth. His lips pulled and tugged at the rough, puckered flesh, his tongue teasing and licking as the tension within her mounted. Her mind turned to mush and the world around them vanished as his hands slid through her hair, tilting her head for a better position. The rhythm of the cool water lapped up against them, thrusting him against her. She barely noticed as the stucco wall scraped her bare back.

He slipped her bathing suit bottom over to the side and his thumb grazed her sex. Fire shot through her belly. His tongue continued to master her mouth as he massaged her, his thumb stroking and fingers probing as his mouth covered her moans. Her fingers curled into his wet, disheveled hair.

She was lost as he assaulted her senses, bringing her pleasure with each twist of his finger. He paused and, unwrapping her legs from his waist, pushed himself away briefly to pull his trunks off and toss them on the ledge.

The water pushed against her exposed swollen

nub, making her body shiver and throb as he untied her suit bottom and tossed it next to his.

Blood zinged through her veins as the ringing in her ears intensified.

Reaching for her under the water, he hooked her legs around his waist. With his hands cupping her hips he plunged into her, burying himself deep within. She cried out as he filled her completely. The water lapped at her as he pulled out briefly and, with a kiss, pushed back inside. The momentum of his thrusts had the water billowing and frothing around them. She reached out and gripped the ledge, giving herself a little more stability as Claude's thrusts continued. The sensation of water between them and all around them had her gasping.

Her arms left the security of the pool's ledge and wrapped around his neck, her fingers gripping the back of his head and slipping through his hair. As their passion intensified, rain began falling around them. The raindrops on her head were as warm as the water that surrounded her.

She cried out as the momentum increased and her orgasm raced through her, setting her nerves on fire as it rushed through her body. Her back arched and she pulled Claude closer. He throbbed inside her as his orgasm followed on the heels of hers. Sated, she rested her head on his shoulder and took deep breaths as her body vibrated and he pulsated inside her.

Their connection felt stronger when they were away from the farm. Like it was the two of them united against the world. Moments like this in his arms, absorbed with only each other, made her wonder why he still held her at arms' length sometimes.

CHAPTER 10

Friendly Arrivals

Sophie

S ophie shifted where she was perched at the edge of her bed, her mobile phone pressed against her ear. She picked at the little lint balls on the silk comforter underneath. "Will you come to the museum with us?" she asked.

"*Non.* You should spend some time with your friends. You haven't seen them in a couple of years. I can always meet them at the party."

"Really?" Sophie ground her teeth. "It's bad enough that you string me along instead of marrying me now that we are grown, but you are going to punish my friends, too?"

"Sophie, be reasonable. You can come and go as you please. It's not so simple for me."

"Now who's being unreasonable? Spending a day with my father and my friends isn't asking for much."

"I never said it was. I just have work to do."

"Whatever." Disappointed that Claude once again avoided spending time with her, Sophie hung up the phone and dropped it beside her. She flung herself back on the bed and closed her eyes with a sigh. It didn't take much for them to be at odds with each other these days. While they'd been away, they'd reconnected. She felt his love and his commitment to her. But now, back in reality, the connection between them seemed frayed again. This made her heart hurt for the way it was.

* * * *

Sophie's feet shuffled and she wrung her hands as her father wrapped his arm around her. The airplane hangar was enormous. The air floated around them, colder under the metal roof as she waited for the plane to finish its landing procedures.

"How about a friendly little wager?"

"Hmm. What's that, Papa?"

"Now with two small children—"

Sophie's laughter was shrill in the metal tube of a building they were in. "Papa, I'm sure even with children, her luggage count will be less."

Bertrand patted her shoulder. "What's got you acting like a Nervous Nelly?"

"Just excited to see the babies."

"Addison, too, I hope."

"Of course, Papa. I think my clock is ticking faster, that's all. I need a dose of cuteness to settle it down again."

"Your time will come, darling. Don't rush it. Enjoy these last moments of freedom, because once you start a family life will never be solely your own ever again."

"Is it really that bad?"

"Not bad, my dear girl. Just different. Your mother and I loved our travels when we first married. The world was our oyster. It was magical."

"Do you regret having me?" Sophie asked, surprised she'd never thought to ask this before. Now there was a sudden dread in her gut at what his response might be.

"Of course not. We had hoped for a house full of kids, but that wasn't in the cards. Once you came we didn't want to leave you behind, and yet you were too young to be carted all over the world. So for the first couple of years, we stayed put. That's all I'm saying. Life changes. Your priorities change. And you are happy when they do. So enjoy the life you have for every day you have it."

"Fair enough, Papa."

Just then Addison exited the airplane and made her way down the steps, her daughter perched on her hip. Her husband Sergei followed, his son dangling over his shoulders in a fireman's hold. Sophie rushed across the apron to them. The advantage of a private plane in a private hangar was that she didn't have to share this moment with dozens of strangers.

The copper highlights in her friend's hair glowed in the bright lights, and was much longer than before.

"*Mon amie*!" Sophie called out.

"Sophie!" Addison squealed, rushing into Sophie's arms.

Sergei stepped up to shake Bertrand's hand. "*Bonjour,* sir."

Bertrand enveloped Sergei in a tight embrace. "Welcome—no need for formalities."

Sergei laughed as Bertrand snagged Maxim from him. "Here, let me lighten that load for you."

Sergei chuckled as he caught Addison's eye.

Sophie envied their easy bond. It didn't seem like she'd ever have that if Claude got his way.

"It's been too long, my friend," Addison said.

"It's about time I met my goddaughter," Sophie said.

"Let me introduce you to my daughter, Natalya Jasmine Leanne Petrova."

"What a mouthful for such a beautiful little girl."

"Well, with three grandmothers it was bound to be."

Laughing, she hugged her friend again, then snagged the child from Addison's arms and started cooing, "Ah, there you are. Open those pretty eyes for Aunt Sophie." Natalya's hazel eyes popped open wide and her cheeks showed off spectacular dimples.

Addison grinned. "You're a natural."

She directed her beaming smile toward her friend for a moment. Turning her attention back to Natalya, Sophie headed for the car.

"Sophie, wait," Addison called out.

"What?" Sophie asked.

"We need the car seats," Sergei said.

"*Non,* we have seats," Sophie said as she continued to walk to the car.

"What?"

"We weren't sure how it would work in the town

car, and we didn't want to take a chance there would be problems. So we bought some and had them installed already. The ones you brought can be used for your strollers or whatever," Sophie said.

"You've thought of everything. Thank you."

"Ah, you're family. And this is supposed to be like a mini vacation for you."

The look of love on her friends' faces as they smiled at her filled her heart with joy. This was what it was all about. Being able to do these little things that made life easier for others was what mattered most to her. She tucked Natalya into the furthest seat, buckling her in before she settled onto the opposite bench.

Her father snapped Maxim into his new seat before ruffling the dark wavy hair on the boy's head. Then he slipped back out of the car and helped Hugo haul the luggage from the plane and stuff it into the second car they'd brought.

"Sophie, darling," Bertrand called out.

"*Oui*, Papa?"

"You were right, of course." Bertrand chuckled. It echoed from his position near the trunk of the second car.

Sophie let out a hearty laugh. "Did you doubt me, Papa?"

Bertrand laughed. "Never, my girl."

"Good, you can take us out to lunch," Sophie called back to him.

"What was that about?" Addison asked.

Sophie waved her hand in the air in a gesture of dismissal. "Ah, nothing. Papa and I made a bet about your luggage, that's all."

Addison directed a questioning look at Sophie.

Sergei pursed his lips. "What is wrong with our luggage?" he asked.

"Not a thing. Papa and I were joking that even with a husband and two small children, she would still bring less luggage than me for the same trip."

Sergei caught his wife's eye. Addison shrugged in response.

"I pack heavy, Addison packs light. Papa and I joked about it."

"I could pack for a small army, for an entire month's stay, and still have room to spare compared to what Sophie packs for herself for a weekend away," Addison explained.

He narrowed his eyes. "*Non*, I don't believe it. No one packs that much extra." His flawless French mingled with English.

Sophie and Addison exchanged a look and giggled. Sergei shook his head.

Addison reached over and took Sergei's hand in

hers. They sat together on the bench across from the car seats, their attention on the children who had quickly fallen asleep once they were secured into their seats.

"We've planned a nice dinner at the apartment tonight, to let you relax. And tomorrow we figured you might enjoy a visit to The Louvre," Sophie said.

"The kids won't behave well enough to visit the museum, I'm afraid," Addison said.

Sergei laughed. "No, they are little Tasmanian Devils."

"They get to spend the day at the farm with Carson and Marte, and the ponies."

"Ponies?" Addison asked.

"*Mon Dieu*, will you trust me? They will be safe."

"We trust you," Sergei affirmed.

"Okay, I'll put my children's lives in your hands," Addison said.

Sophie laughed. "*Mon amie*, you will not regret it. You deserve some adult time as well."

"Sounds good to me. I'm exhausted," Addison said.

Sergei lifted their entwined hands and kissed the back of hers. Addison smiled and leaned her head against his shoulder.

"Tonight, we relax. We'll have dinner at *Le Meurice*

tomorrow. The ceremony is Friday evening, with the celebration right after."

Addison nodded. "Sounds wonderful."

Sophie laughed. Addison had never been a bundle full of energy like herself. Then again, even if she had been in the past, the exhaustion of chasing two little ones had to wear a person out.

CHAPTER 11

Domestic Bliss

Sophie

The following morning, Sophie was up bright and early, excited to see the children. She dressed quickly before sneaking into the small bedroom across from her friends, finding the children quietly giggling in the darkened room.

Pausing in the doorway, Sophie beamed. This, this was what she wanted, what she dreamed of having with Claude. Giggling children, a loving husband, her own little family surrounding her. Turning towards the windows Sophie sighed wistfully.

She opened the heavy damask drapes with a flourish, flooding the room with light. Maxim stood on his bed and wobbled.

"Breakie?" he asked.

"Breakfast, yes, let's do that. How's your nappy? Do you need a change?"

At the quizzical glance he gave her, she gathered he had no idea what she had asked.

"Let's change your diaper first," she suggested.

"Wet," Maxim said, his mouth puckered.

"Okay, then, let's get you out of that."

Maxim didn't need any further encouragement. He dropped his pajama bottoms, including the soggy pull-up, and stood bare-bottomed on his bed, jumping up and down like a spring.

"No more diapie! Diapie gone!" he crowed.

With a barely contained laugh, Sophie picked up the wet pull-up and tossed it in the can before she scrounged through the huge blue diaper bag with elephants and other zoo animals on it. Pulling out a pair of regular children's underwear, she slipped them onto the boy before pulling his pajama bottoms back on.

Natalya stood on unsteady legs in her travel playpen, two tiny hands gripping the soft edges. Her eyes grew wide with curiosity.

Once she pulled her out of her makeshift crib, Sophie made quick work of changing her diaper before dressing her back in her nightgown. With Maxim's little hand in hers and Natalya on her hip, she went downstairs as he chatted the entire way.

Her father was already in the dining room, she learned, as Maxim released her hand and tore into the room, loudly expressing his delight in finding Bertrand seated at the table.

By the time she caught up, Maxim was already planted in her father's lap, pounding his little hands on the placemat, vibrating the china cup in its saucer.

"Papa."

"*Bonjour*." He rang a little bell on the table beside his coffee cup.

Moments later Agnes came through the door, followed by Hugo, bearing plates of fun- shaped pancakes, with fruit bowls and a large bowl of fresh whipped cream.

"Oh, Papa, they are going to love this."

"I know." Bertrand grinned.

Maxim dug in and immediately had fruit, whipped cream, and syrup all over the table in front of him and down the front of his pajamas. Sophie's eyes grew wide as she watched the mess progress. And her father's stoic response.

"I think he likes it," Bertrand said.

Addison and Sergei walked into the room just as Natalya pulled her hands from the messy goo on

Sophie's plate, and slid those sticky hands into her mahogany-colored hair.

"Ooh." Addison rushed to Sophie's seat and leaned down to reach for the squirming child.

Sophie swatted Addison's hand away. "Don't you dare, she's just fine. Go sit by Papa and Maxim." She was enjoying the morning's shenanigans with the kids and wanted to soak up as much as she could before they were gone again.

Her attention was diverted from Addison as Maxim bounced in his seat. "Daddy!"

"My boy, what have you got there?" Sergei asked.

Maxim grinned as his goo-covered hand waved in response.

Sergei chuckled as Addison shook her head, and he joined his wife on the far side of the table. He patted her hand and smiled.

Bertrand had Maxim giggling up a storm, while Sophie finished feeding Natalya.

"Today the children will play at the stables, and we shall visit the museum and have a grown-up day together. *Oui*?" Sophie asked.

"Sure, that sounds relaxing. Will we be home for dinner?" Addison asked.

"*Oui*," Bertrand replied.

"*Magnifique!*" Sophie said. Natalya squirmed in

her lap as she wiped the child's sticky fingers off before they went back in her hair. Sophie wasn't winning this battle, it seemed. The dry cloth napkin wasn't much help. "*Zut Alors*, how can you get so sticky, so quickly, *petite fille*?"

Sergei laughed. "It's a special talent."

"I'll get her cleaned up," Addison said, setting her napkin down on the table.

"*Non*, sit. Eat. I've got her," Sophie said.

The housekeeper walked in and her lips twitched, her amusement barely contained. "*Mademoiselle*, would you like some assistance?"

"*Oui*, Agnes, if you could take her, I'll carry *Monsieur* Maxim. It looks like he is in need of a bath as well."

"Well, my boy looks like you're in for it." Sergei chuckled.

Maxim's face twisted into a scowl as his lips protruded. "No bath." He shook his head violently.

"I have bubbles, and rubber duckies, and sailboats for you to play with, *Monsieur* Maxeem," Sophie said.

"Boats?" Maxim's head stopped swiveling, his eyes lit up, and a wide grin split his face. He lifted his arms in ready agreement to be picked up.

"Ah, you're so good with them, Sophie," Addison said.

"Yes, bribery works wonders on little monsters," Sergei agreed.

Sophie bustled the kids out of the dining room while Addison and Sergei finished their breakfast and chatted with her father.

Once upstairs, kneeling beside the tub, she poured a massive amount of bubble bath into the empty tub. The large tub began to immediately fill with thick clouds of fragrant white bubbles as she turned the faucet on warm. Agnes came in with an arm full of thick cotton towels and set them on the counter. Sophie waved her hand under the fluffy foam to test the water before she set the kids down beneath the growing mound of bubbles.

"Why so many towels for just the two of them?" Sophie asked.

Agnes grinned. "*Humph*, you will see."

Within moments, there was just as much water on the floor as there was left in the tub. The front of their shirts, their hair, and the floor were covered in bubbles. Twenty minutes later the tub was emptied, the bubbles rinsed off the children and down the drain, and the two women were giggling as they tried to wrangle a slippery, waterlogged little girl out of the tub. Maxim continued to press himself against the back of the tub, stubbornly refusing to get out.

"Maxeem, darling, you can take the boat out of the tub and play with it," Sophie said.

This seemed to pacify him, and he scooted forward while continuing to clutch the toy boat in his hand. Sophie wrapped the towel around his wet body and pulled him from the tub.

"Well, that was certainly easier the second time around." Sophie sighed as she dropped Maxim's bundled form onto her lap. *Lesson learned. Wrap a towel around them before pulling them out.*

Agnes smiled as she rubbed down Natalya and carried her into the bedroom. "Your time with my grandkids has taught you well."

Sophie lifted Maxim to his feet before scrambling to stand herself. "Come, little Maxeem, let's get you ready to see the ponies today."

"Ponieez!" Maxim squealed as he tore from the bathroom, leaving the towel in a pile on the floor.

With an exaggerated breath, Sophie mopped the water from the floor with the extra towels Agnes had the foresight to bring. They certainly were messy little things. But that did not deter her in the least.

Dropping the heavy, sopping towels into the tub, she made her way to the bedroom just as Addison came through the main door from the hallway.

"Mommee!" Natalya shrieked.

"How's my little monkey? Wet, I see," Addison said.

Maxim sat on the floor playing with his boat, ignoring all efforts to get him dressed.

"Do they have running shoes?" Sophie asked.

"Running shoes? These little terrors don't need no stinking running shoes." Addison nuzzled a squirming Natalya as she spoke. Natalya squeaked in response.

"For the stables," Sophie said.

"Ah. Yes, sneakers would be good for that. Should we put them in boots?"

"Ponieez," Maxim said, looking up from his boat.

"*Non*, I have a surprise for them when they get there," Sophie said.

"Sophie," Addison warned.

Sophie shrugged. "I own the finest stables in all of France, and you expected me not to properly dress my godchildren? *Humph!*"

"What is this about dressing the children?" Sergei asked as he entered the room.

"Oh, Sophie is being overly dramatic as usual," Addison said.

Sophie beamed at them with what she considered a win. There would be no more talk about the children's new riding gear that had been made for them. It was to be a surprise.

Sergei looked back and forth between her and his wife, clearly not understanding the conversation, then shrugged, and picked his son up off the floor.

Sophie laughed as Sergei turned the boy upside down on his shoulder and spun his naked little body up in the air.

"So, my boy, are we getting dressed today?" he asked.

"No!" Maxim yelled out.

"You cannot go outside and play with the ponies without pants on," Sergei said seriously.

"I can't?" Maxim queried, winded from the spin.

Slowing down, Sergei twisted the boy's body until his son's face looked at his. "No, naked little boys cannot ride ponies, so do not give your mama a hard time now. Get dressed so you can go play."

"Yes, Papa."

"I've got them, Sir and Madame. I will get them dressed while you get ready," Agnes said.

"I could grow to like this," Sergei said.

Addison laughed. "I just bet you could."

With a loud smacking sound, Sergei kissed his son on the cheek and set the boy down.

Addison kissed Natalya and leaned her over to let Sergei do the same before she handed her over to

Agnes and bent down and kissed the top of Maxim's head. "Be a good boy today."

Agnes secured Natalya on her hip and reached for Maxim's hand, and the three of them exited the bedroom.

"Let's meet downstairs in an hour," Sophie suggested.

Addison and Sergei nodded as he reached for her hand, and they walked into their bedroom on the other side of the hall.

CHAPTER 12

Another Day in Paris

Sophie

Sophie exited her room at the same moment that Addison was making her way down the stairs. "Wait up," she called out.

"Is your boyfriend joining us today?" Addison asked as she paused on the first step.

"*Non*, not today," Sophie said.

"I look forward to meeting him."

"Yeah, if he can bother to make time for it."

"Sophie, give the guy a break. You're young, you have plenty of time."

"Says the woman already married with two beautiful babies," she muttered.

"Yeah, but I wasn't always cooperative either.

Sergei had to have patience with me, just like you need to have with Claude."

"He had help."

"Yes, he had a devious matchmaker." She looked pointedly at Sophie. "Is that what you need? Someone to push Claude into marrying you, even if he's not ready?"

"*Non*. But..." Sophie stomped her foot.

"What's with the stomping?" Sergei asked as he came up behind them.

"Sophie thinks it's your turn to be the matchmaker, since she came to your rescue last time." Once he joined her on the stairs, Addison wrapped her arm through his and laughed.

Sergei chuckled. "Sure, should I secretly plan your wedding and then drag him kicking and screaming to the altar? Or did you have something else in mind?" He reached out and tugged Sophie's hair.

Sophie's eyes grew wide. "I hadn't thought of that."

"No." Sergei and Addison sputtered simultaneously.

Sophie grinned. "I wouldn't, though it's not a bad plan, all things considered." *Then again, it might be necessary.*

"Ugh," Addison groaned.

Sergei laughed as they began descending the stairs.

"You will meet him at the graduation ceremony, or at the party at the big house after," Sophie said.

Addison nodded and made her way down the stairs. Bertrand was at the bottom, glancing at his phone as they reached the first floor of the apartment.

"Ah, there you are. Ready?" Bertrand asked as he put his phone back into his inside coat pocket.

"*Oui*, Papa." Sophie nodded and walked through the door her father held open, out to the elevators.

Downstairs, their car was ready and Hugo stood at attention at the open back door. Sophie climbed in, followed by Addison and Sergei. "Good morning, James," Bertrand said to the doorman, slipping into the car last. James tipped his hat as Hugo closed the door.

Settled in, Sophie gripped Addison's hand. "I'm so glad you are here."

"Us too." Addison squeezed her hand in return.

The car zipped through traffic like a breeze. The sun was shining, not a cloud in the sky. It was going to be a lovely day.

Sophie peppered Addison with questions about the children while Sergei talked with Bertrand about the horses.

When the car pulled up to the side street of The Louvre, Hugo opened the door and helped them out.

"*Merci,*" Bertrand said, exiting the car.

Sophie beamed as she led the way through the maze of people to the waiting docent for their private tour.

"I have a surprise for you, *moy drook.*" She caught Addison's gaze. It brought her such joy to be able to do something special for her friends.

Addison's brow rose, clearly understanding this would be a gift for Sergei since Sophie had spoken in Russian.

"Hmm, Miss Sophie. More of your secrets?" Sergei laughed.

"I promise you will be pleased," she replied.

"I always am, *mon amie.*"

The docent, a teenaged, flaxen-haired boy in a dark coat, walked up to them. "*Monsieur* Compte, welcome. It is good to see you again, sir. And you, *Mademoiselle*. If you and your guests are ready, please follow me." He led them through a throng of people to the main area.

Bertrand placed his hand on Addison's back and guided her to move in front of him as they passed through the door. Once inside, Sophie walked beside her father while Addison took Sergei's hand.

They followed the docent through the corridor and into an enormous room with large, gild-framed artwork. The first impression one got was that they were old. The frames made it clear the paintings were done in the Neo-Classical style.

Sophie stepped up behind her friend and placed her chin on Addison's shoulder. "Hmm." She stepped back and a wide grin split her face.

Sergei slipped his arm around Addison's waist and took a closer look at the sign. His eyes grew wide as he took in the message.

"Oh," he said.

The plaque read *Russian Impressionism, Symbolism, and Neo-Classical Art Collection.* Under it in smaller print: *On tour from the Russian Armoury:*

Joseph Josefovich Charlemagne, Ice Fair on the Neva River (1860)

Mikhail Vrubel, Venice, Bridge of Sighs (1893) and Six-Winged Seraph (1904)

Boris Kustodiev, Lilac (1906)

Konstantin Somov, Mocked Kiss (1908)

Valentin Serov, Portrait of Princess Olga Orlova (1911)

Nikolai Kalmakov, Artemis and the Sleeping Endymion (1917)

"I thought you might be getting homesick by now," Sophie said, feeling especially pleased with herself.

There was a portable wall positioned in the center of the room, where various artwork was displayed as a focal point.

"*Spasibo*," he whispered and squeezed her hand.

Sophie beamed. She wanted to show her appreciation for their coming to Paris for her ceremony.

As Sergei continued to take in the paintings they walked around the room, hands clasped.

"We've been talking about taking the kids to see the family for Christmas," Addison whispered into her ear.

"That would be lovely. But a long flight with the children..." Sophie said.

"Yes, that's the concern I've been mulling over."

Sophie laughed. "I don't envy you, but I think it would do them all good."

"Do what? Who?" Sergei asked as he wrapped his arm around his wife's shoulder.

"She was just telling me about your plans for Christmas in Saint Petersburg," Sophie said.

Sergei's lips pursed, and his brow rose. "Did we decide then?"

"Apparently so." Addison nodded.

"Okay, then I will let the family know." Sergei's eyes lit up as he kissed her cheek.

They continued to peruse the paintings around them. The collection of Russian art was limited. It was relatively rare to have items from Russian artists in The Louvre, so there wasn't much left to see. Their group made the rounds through the small section of the Denon Wing.

"I'm famished. Are we ready for lunch?" Sophie asked.

Sergei chuckled. "You wore most of your breakfast this morning."

"Natalya had the rest in her hair," Addison said.

"Pretty much," Sophie agreed. The image of a messy little girl in her lap, putting her goo- covered hands through her hair, flashed through her mind. She had no regrets. They were precious moments. Sophie longed to have children of her own to fill her mornings with more sticky memories, and she wanted them to be Claude's.

"Earth to Sophie." Addison waved her hand in front of Sophie's face.

Shaking herself out of her reverie, Sophie focused on her friend. "*Pardon.*" Turning to where her father stood she called out, "Papa, are you ready for lunch, or do you need a few minutes?"

Bertrand left the docent and stepped closer to their little group. "Lunch sounds lovely," he said.

Sophie hooked her arm through her father's. He patted her hand as he led the way out of the room.

They took their time, slowly ambling through the corridors as they made their way out of the museum. After lunch, they all climbed into the car to head to the stables to see the children. Sophie was already missing their sweet smiles and squirming bodies. Claude had better get himself organized quickly, because her biological clock was practically screeching in her ear.

She hoped to be gloriously fat and happy before she was thirty. She imagined this that is what being settled would look like. And if that was to happen, he needed to get her down the aisle in the next two years. Since it would take her at least a year to plan the wedding then, by her calculations, he only had until the holidays to make his move.

Looking out the car window, Sophie was lost in her own world. She practically had it all mapped out in her mind.

"Sophie?" Addison asked. "You're a million miles away."

"*Pardon.* Thinking of little Maxeem in his new riding habit." The lie rolled easily off her tongue.

Sergei laughed and shook his head.

Addison rolled her eyes. "Well, at least you didn't buy one for Nat as well."

Bertrand chuckled.

"What?" Addison asked, pursing her lips.

"Well, strictly speaking, I didn't buy any clothes for Maxeem, or Natalya," she said.

"What does strictly speaking mean?" Addison narrowed her eyes at Sophie.

"They were custom made, of course," Bertrand said.

"How could that be?" Addison asked.

"Well, the same clothier who makes the clothes for the jockeys agreed to make a miniature set for the children," Sophie said.

"Whoa! Now, wait a minute. I never agreed to having Natalya on a horse. She's barely three, Sophie."

"Don't worry, the baby will be properly dressed—" Bertrand said.

Addison shook her head violently.

Bertrand put his hand on her arm. "But I promise you, she will not be placed on a horse to ride."

"What does that mean exactly?"

"Trust me. We would never put the children at risk," Sophie said.

Addison leaned into her husband's side, and he wrapped his arm around her. "Have no fear, *lyublyu*. I trust Sophie to know what's safe for the children. Bertrand, too."

"Thank you. You won't be disappointed," Bertrand said.

Sophie held Addison's other hand and relaxed. Her friend would love what she'd done when she saw it with her own eyes.

Once they reached the property, Addison's anxiety was up again. Sophie could see the tension in her friend's shoulders. The way she squeezed Sergei's hand gave some indication as well. Maybe she should have shared her intentions with them before. But she had been so excited, the plans just ran away with her. And now it was coming back to bite her.

She grinned as Marte came from the back of the house, pushing an old-fashioned buggy that had been used for all of the children in her father's family. It brought back so many memories.

After getting out of the car Addison practically flew, her sandals barely touching the graveled path between the car and where Marte was pushing Natalya.

She slid to a stop just inches away. Reaching into

the covered stroller she pulled out the little girl, attired like a miniature jockey, with her perfectly sized helmet fastened to her head. Natalya was dressed in a button-up beige shirt, with a tailor-made eggplant jacket and charcoal-gray breeches. Her bangs smashed down on her forehead, and black leather riding boots ended just below her knees.

"Wow. Look at you, my precious girl." Sergei reached over and plucked his daughter from her mother's arms and gave her a quick squeeze.

"Mommee!" Maxim came tearing out of the barn as fast as his stubby legs could carry him. He launched himself into his mother's arms. "Dressed for ponieez!" His helmet barely missed hitting her square in the eye, instead smacking right into her cheekbone.

Addison flinched, but grinned at his enthusiasm.

"So you are, my boy. So you are," Sergei said as he reached over and pretended to steal his son's nose before he caressed his wife's cheek. A thin red line had begun to appear where the edge of the helmet had collided.

Maxim giggled and squirmed in his mother's arms. She kissed his forehead and set him back down.

His outfit, like his sister's, was expertly fitted to his small frame. Navy riding breeches were tucked into his leather boots at the knee, topped by a steel-blue competition jacket. The gray button-up shirt underneath already had creases in it from his adventures.

Maxim sauntered over to Sophie and hugged her leg.

Sophie leaned down and picked up the little boy, settling him on her hip just as Claude came around the corner.

CHAPTER 13

Biological Clocks

Claude

Claude had his head in the clouds, thinking of Sophie. Coming around the back of the barn he stopped, seeing Sophie standing near the front of the house with the little boy on her hip, surrounded by a group of people.

The way Sophie stood, beaming down at that little face, made his heart skip a beat. He would love to see her holding his son that way. *Someday.* He shook his head and made his way over to her. Now wasn't the time to get all sentimental about their future. There were things that needed to be done first.

"*Bonjour,*" he said.

"Claude, meet Addison and Sergei. From America," Sophie said as she reached out to him.

"Ponieez!" Maxim pointed a stubby little finger at Claude.

"*Oui,* I just came from there!" Claude said. He came and shook the little finger that was pointing at him. "And who might you be?"

"That little handful is our son, Maxim," Addison said.

"Ponieez!"

"We haven't made it down to the stables yet," Marte said. "We just managed to get them dressed in their new outfits. Boots on little wiggling toes are a bit of a handful." She grinned at Maxim.

"Ah, that explains your impatience, little man. Of course, we'll go see the ponies now." Sophie nuzzled Maxim's cheek.

As everyone made their way towards the stables, Claude caught up with Bertrand. "Sir, a moment?"

"*Oui?*" Bertrand asked.

"I'm concerned about Jezebel. I think she is not taking Balthazar's departure well."

"Is she eating?" Bertrand slowed his pace.

"Not as much as she was. She's lost a little weight over the last week."

"Okay, let's go take a look."

Claude continued to fill him in on the horse's condition as they fell in line behind everyone heading to the stables. His heart swelled, watching Sophie talk to the boy. Bouncing him on her hip, and making him smile. She looked like she was born to be a mother. Shaking the thought from his head, movement in his peripheral vision caught his attention.

It was Jacques. *Hmm. That's strange.* He could have sworn the trainers had already left for the day. Then again, maybe he had stayed around to visit his mother. If that was the case, who was he to question it? He only wanted his mother's happiness. And if she fell in love again and re-married, a huge burden would be lifted from his shoulders.

"So, could it be colic?" Bertrand asked.

"Hmm. I'm sorry, what?"

"Jezebel. Are you thinking colic?"

"No, I think it is just a reaction to Balthazar leaving. Their stalls were side by side. And the trainers socialized them together often. But I could be wrong."

"How about her teeth?"

"Her teeth are sound, and so are her hooves," Claude said.

Bertrand nodded.

They split from the group and continued past

them. Jezebel was in her stall, head hanging over the wooden gate. She bobbed her head and backed up.

"There, there; how's my girl doing?" Bertrand stepped into the stall and patted her neck. She pushed her head into his hand.

"What's her current diet?" he asked.

Claude pulled the clipboard off the tack on the board just outside her stall. "According to this, she's getting four flakes of timothy hay and two pounds of grain."

"Any suggestions?"

"We could try a slow approach. Give her a mix of timothy hay and alfalfa, and add a supplement, leaving the grain as is. We should also pull back on her training routine for a week. And then reassess. We'll know it's working if she gains her weight back. We are also moving Goliath over to be next to her."

"I like the way you think. Let's do that and we'll see how she does."

Claude nodded just as Sophie and the rest joined them.

"Is everything all right with Jez?" she asked.

"*Oui*. Fine. All is good," Bertrand said. "Max, would you like to sit on her?"

"Ride. Ponieez!"

Everyone laughed. His exuberance was contagious.

Claude placed a blanket over the back of the horse and Bertrand picked up Maxim and settled his little legs on either side of her. Jezebel flicked her ears, her only outward sign of acknowledging the stall full of people. She was an unusually calm filly, so being the center of attention didn't bother her.

"Yippee!" Maxim bounced up and down while Bertrand held his arm.

Addison pulled a small digital camera from her purse and snapped a couple of pictures of Maxim astride the chestnut filly.

"Why don't we put Nat up there with her brother?" Sergei asked.

All eyes turned toward Bertrand and Maxim.

"Maxeem, will you take a picture with your sister on the pony?" Sophie asked.

"Ponieez, piktures!" Maxim squealed. He bounced and Bertrand had to maneuver the boy around to keep him from slipping. It was the perfect opportunity to scoot his little body back to make room for Natalya.

"May I?" Claude asked Sergei as he extended his hands toward Natalya.

"Of course," Sergei said.

Claude took the girl from Sergei and tossed her in the air until she was a fit of giggles. Addison snapped a few pictures of her flying in the air before he placed Natalya on the horse in front of her brother.

He stood on one side of the horse, holding Natalya steady, while Bertrand was on the other side in the back, holding a wiggling Maxim. The children looked like the perfect pair of riders astride a beautiful filly.

This image imprinted in his mind, and the urge to settle down and have children with Sophie was paramount. He glanced over at her as she laughed and took pictures of the kids. She was happier than he'd seen her in days. She was positively beaming.

Damn, I love that woman.

His heart felt ready to burst. He wanted nothing more than to pull her into his arms and kiss her breathless. But she was still standoffish, so he knew there was still a bridge to cross before things were back to normal. *I just can't seem to win.*

CHAPTER 14

Champagne and Celebrations

Sophie

Sophie had gotten ready early, which was no small feat with two rambunctious little ones who weren't easily manipulated into dressing up for the occasion. The amount of bribery that it took was staggering.

Bertrand and Sophie settled in for a quick drink in the parlor while they waited for everyone else to be ready. The children were dressed, and surprisingly clean after the mess with the treats she'd plied them with to get their cooperation.

"Stop pouting, girl," Bertrand said.

"I'm not." Sophie's lip protruded.

"How is it, my girl, I know the two of you better than you know yourselves?" Bertrand asked.

Sophie shrugged.

"You need to spread your wings and he needs roots."

"That makes no sense. He already has roots here, and I have spread my wings. I've spent years away studying. Boarding schools as a child in England and then a year at university in Russia," Sophie said.

"Someday I'll be gone, and this will all be yours. You will eventually run the entire business end. The breeding is only a small part of the world you will take over."

"That day won't come for many years. There is still plenty of time before then." Sophie stared at her father. She steadfastly refused to consider a world without him in it.

"I plan to step down in a few years and hand the reins to you and Claude. For now, you have plenty of options. You can even see outside clients and experience it all, if you want. Claude needs to be his own man and to feel independent."

"And giving him the title of head vet does that?" Sophie said, biting her lip.

"Isn't CEO an even heavier burden?" Bertrand

countered. "You expect too much of yourselves and each other."

"I don't want that responsibility," Sophie said, a stubborn set to her shoulders.

"You will always be a vet, especially in charge of all breeding selections. And one day you and Claude will be making all of the financial ones and ownership ones, too. So, don't begrudge him this. He should have a piece of the pie that is just his, not just as your partner. He's earned that, too, you know."

Merde, I'm so selfish sometimes.

"Oh, Papa, you're right, of course." Shame flooded her cheeks. Her father only saw the best possibilities for her and Claude.

"Now go kiss and make up."

Sophie nodded, and wiped a tear from the corner of her eye. She slipped from the room and out of the house, not ready yet to play nice. Though she should congratulate Claude. He, too, had been working toward this almost his entire life.

Oui, Claude deserved it. He had worked hard for it. Though it might bring his dreams closer to reality, she feared it would not bring him closer to her.

. . .

While everyone was in the parlor, sipping their drinks before they left for the ceremony, Sophie stood on the back porch for a moment of peace and some fresh air. Her father's words stung. He was right, of course, but it didn't hurt any less to be reminded that those she loved didn't seem to see her. She was more sensitive than usual lately, the lack of sleep only adding to the tension in her shoulders. Unfailingly, the days were longer and the nights lonelier when she and Claude were at odds.

"So, what has you so stressed, my friend?" Sergei asked as he joined her at the railing.

"I don't sleep well when Claude and I are bickering. The nightmares sneak in."

"Nightmares?"

"Sometimes I dream of Russia."

"Of Russia?" Sergei's confusion was evident by the squinted eyes and furrowed brow he directed at her.

"Of the attack. It's not that big a deal." She tried to reassure him. Her voice lowered. "It's not all the time, just when I'm extra stressed."

"What does your Claude say?"

"He doesn't know. Neither does Papa."

"Why ever not?" Sergei choked out.

"I'm ashamed."

"*Mon amie*, there is nothing to be ashamed of. It

wasn't your fault. You must not shoulder that burden, and certainly not alone without support," Sergei said.

Sophie shook her head. "You don't understand. There are women you play with and women you take home to your mother."

"I do not know that saying."

"It means there are women you date or have sex with, and those you bring home to meet your family because you are going to marry them," Sophie said.

"But you've already met his mother." Sergei's nose scrunched as he waited for her response.

"That's not the point. I don't want Claude to ever question my worth. To doubt that I'm his future."

"And you think being assaulted will change his opinion of you? I'm not so sure this Claude fellow is worthy of you if that's the case." He narrowed his eyes at her.

Sophie patted his hand. "Not being attacked. But where I was and why I was there when I was attacked. I wasn't on my way home from studying at the library. I was at an illegal underground club. And it hadn't been my first time in one. Though that was the only time I was at one being raided by the Gestapo."

Sergei chuckled. "They aren't the Gestapo. That was Nazi Germany. Russia has regular *Politsiya* like everyone else. You know that."

"Yeah, yeah. They don't act like everyone else and you know it."

Sergei shrugged. "They are less lenient than the police in America, that's for sure."

"The point is that I was angry and wild while I was away. I understand now that all I really need is Claude. He balances me and makes me a better person."

"So tell him. Make him understand."

"I can't. I can't risk him turning away from me."

"What makes you think he would do that?"

"Because I was angry with him when I left for Russia. I had grown tired of waiting for him to do it, so I proposed to him instead. He said no." Sophie flushed with shame at the memory. "The humiliation was too much so I ran. I told papa I was going to Russia and went. He pulled some strings to get me a last-minute place at the school and in the dorms and, because of that, I met you and Addison."

Sophie looked imploringly at Sergei, "Do you see why I couldn't tell him now? I was somewhere I shouldn't have been, doing something I shouldn't have been, all because I was mad at him and acting out. All it got me was hurt and humiliated further."

"Oh, Sophie, anyone worthy of you wouldn't turn their back on you simply because you were hurt. Regardless of where you were. Or why. You think about that. You deserve to have someone who stands by you no matter what."

Sergei kissed her cheek and went back into the house, leaving her to mull over his advice. More than anything, she needed Claude to see her as an independent woman. As an equal. Not a damsel in distress. And certainly never a victim.

———

Sophie glanced around the room as she waited for her turn to climb the stairs to the stage. Claude stood behind her in line, three people back, as it was arranged alphabetically. Her father sat in the front row of the bleachers, Addison next to him, laughing at something Bertrand said. Sergei was beside her, holding her hand, their daughter on his lap, their son standing between them, squirming in place.

Claude's mother sat on the other side of her father. Agnes and Marte sat on the bench directly behind them, sharing this moment with her and Claude. The women had practically raised them during their time at the stables.

Her nerves were in overdrive over the party back at the farmhouse. Dozens of their closest friends would be attending. Sophie hoped that Marte would forgive her eventually for the insult of having it catered and staffed, so that she could participate and relax for an evening. It had taken expert negotiating skills to soothe Marte's ruffled feathers. Though used to the large parties and the caterers, what she wholeheartedly disapproved of was taking the night off and the back seat to managing the affair.

The love coming from them was intense. And so welcome. That everyone sat together as a family made her heart swell with pride.

After she crossed the stage and shook her professors' hands, she waited on the other side of the platform for Claude. As he stepped down the stairs, she hugged and kissed him. He kissed her back and laughed.

"Does this mean I'm forgiven?"

"For now. I wish to be happy tonight, and not even you can dim my shine."

"Ah, Sophie, I have no wish to dim you. I just wish you would be patient."

"*Non*, not tonight." She placed a finger against his lips. "I will not have such serious talk. Tonight, we celebrate with our families. We enjoy what we've accomplished so far."

"I like that idea." Claude kissed her again and she led the way back to their seats.

She fidgeted in her seat for the following hour, waiting for the rest of the program to complete. Claude laughed and took her hand.

Now that they had crossed the stage, no one would say much about their switched seats. Holding his hand was a reminder that even when they were upset with each other, he was still there beside her.

The lights blazed as the limousine pulled through the gates. The fence posts had been strung with lights and the trees twinkled with the sparkling strands that had been looped inside their foliage and around their trunks. As the cars came to a stop in front of the house, the windows of the house glowed. Music drifted around them from the band set up on the back patio.

Many of the guests had already arrived, much to Marte's dismay. Sophie watched her stiffen in the seat across from her. Marte abhorred the idea of people roaming through her halls, as she thought of them, when she wasn't there to supervise. She was like a mother hen, expecting to control her environment.

"Marte, you have the night off. Agnes will make sure you behave. You are family, and I want you to celebrate with us for one night. Promise me, please!" Sophie said.

Marte rolled her eyes. Agnes laughed. "*Oui, Mademoiselle*. Tonight, we celebrate. Tomorrow we worry about the mess, Marte?" Agnes nudged Marte's arm.

Marte huffed and glared at her before her stiff shoulders relaxed and she relented. "Fine, for tonight. For you. But if one of my plates gets broken I'll have their heads, I tell you!"

Bertrand chuckled.

"Fair enough. Thank you. Now, let's go party." Sophie unbuckled Maxim from his seat.

"Will she really get angry if any of the china gets broken?" Addison asked.

"Oh, without a doubt. She takes the running of this house seriously. As though each piece of dishware or cutlery comes from her personal collection."

"Ooh."

Sophie winked. "Don't worry. I had the caterers bring supplies. Everything used tonight was rented and will be taken away when the party ends."

"Does Marte know?"

Sophie giggled. "*Non*, she would have complained at the wasted expense. Just as she complains that something might get broken."

Addison nodded. "Should I take him from you?"

"*Non*, Maxim will be my date for the evening." Sophie led the little tuxedo-clad boy toward the dessert table.

"Now, *this* is going to be the most important part of the party." Little brown eyes went wide as he stared at her, glanced back at the table, then again at her. "So Maxim, you have to be on your very best behavior tonight. Can you do that for me?"

Maxim bobbed his little head. Addison caught her eye, grinning widely from a few feet away.

"That's a good boy. So, let's go meet everyone, and once you've had some dinner we will tackle the sweets together, okay?"

More head-bobbing from him, while more grinning came from his mother. Sophie shrugged. All that was needed were some basic boundaries and the offer of a table full of chocolate delicacies to get what she wanted.

Too bad Claude isn't so easily swayed.

CHAPTER 15

A Niggling Feeling

Claude

Claude stood in the back of the room, finally free of the well-wishers who had surrounded him since they returned to the farm. Being the center of attention, even when it was for accolades, made him uncomfortable.

Sophie, on the other hand, was a natural socialite. She was at ease with everyone who had come. Shaking hands and kissing cheeks, while never letting her eyes wander too far from Maxim. The way she was with the children was eye-opening. Not that he'd ever questioned her ability to be a fabulous mother someday. Then again, he hadn't given that much thought either. It was more seeing her in action that brought his attention to the matter. Sophie had vetoed the suggestion to get an attendant to mind the children for the evening, saying that it would keep Marte and Agnes from fussing with the catering if they had the children to manage. Addison had given a specific bedtime and everyone had agreed.

"Thank you," he said, taking a bottle of beer from the passing tray. The tuxedo-clad server nodded as he continued his way around the room. He had never been a fan of Champagne, and he just wasn't in the mood for red wine. If he was honest with himself, he was more concerned about spilling it on someone's lovely dress. He often became all butterfingers when nervous, and large crowds tended to make him uneasy. Beer just seemed a safer bet under the circumstances.

Resting his shoulder against a wall, he was in his element watching Sophie in hers. He imagined that was how they would be together in marriage, him observing her while she made the rounds, making everyone feel included. Sipping his beer, he took in the room full of people. Friends, family, and too many business associates to count. Compte Stables was a powerhouse in the equine world. And Bertrand Compte was the overlord of that empire. While he had no doubt that he would be an asset to the farm, he knew that he could never replace Bertrand, and he had zero desire to ever do so. The people, the business, the entertaining and schmoozing, that was Sophie's domain. And watching her now made that even more evident. Her dress dazzled, her eyes sparkled, she was, as always, a beauty. Her easy confidence shone at times like these.

"What are you doing hiding over here in the corner?" Sergei asked. He offered him another bottle of beer.

Claude drank the dregs of his bottle and set it on the table beside him before accepting the fresh one from Sergei. "I'm trying to avoid the crowd."

"Aren't they here for you?" Sergei asked.

"Yes, though mostly Sophie and Bertrand."

Sergei's brow arched.

"This is not my type of thing. A big party with a lot of people milling about for attention."

Sergei laughed. "I can understand that." They clinked their bottles together. Sergei leaned against the wall beside him. They stood in silence while they drank their beers and people-watched.

Claude's mother bustled about, talking with Marte and Agnes, keeping their attention occupied. The three women were like cackling hens, their faces split with wide grins. Like Sophie, his mother was a natural negotiator. As they came further into the room he noticed Jacques join them, handing his mother a glass of Champagne. While she smiled and thanked him the women excused themselves, leaving the two of them alone.

Claude smiled. He liked the idea of his mother dating again. There wasn't a stitch of jealousy as he watched Jacques huddle close to her ear, whispering something that made her laugh. She hadn't laughed often enough since his father died. It made him happy to see her so content. He would need to get to know Jacques better. Possibly even ridding himself of that unsettling nagging feeling he got every time he saw him. It might help his mother feel more comfortable about dating after being alone so long if she could see that he was pleased with the idea.

He took another deep pull from his beer as he watched Jacques leave his mother and head out the side door.

The guy was likely as uncomfortable as he was in this crowd. Probably went to get some air. It wouldn't hurt to join him for a moment.

"Sergei, can you excuse me for a moment? I need to get some fresh air."

"I'll join you, if you don't mind," Sergei said.

"By all means." Claude stepped away from the corner they were in and made his way out the front door, as it was closer to them. Getting through the tight group of people was key.

Once on the porch, he walked around the house to the side from which he'd watched Jacques exit, yet the man was nowhere to be found. For a man walking with a pronounced limp, he managed to disappear into thin air when it suited him. *Where did he go so fast?*

With a shrug, he sat on the wooden bench up against the house and took another swig of his beer. Sergei leaned against the railing, facing him.

"Do you enjoy life on the farm?" Sergei asked.

"I do. And you? What keeps your days busy?"

"My wife and I both work at a university as science professors."

"Interesting. You work together?" Claude asked.

"Different disciplines, and different buildings, but same school."

Claude nodded. "So, how long are you and your family planning to be in France?"

"I believe we are expected to stay until next Wednesday," Sergei said.

"That's a nice little holiday for the kids."

"They are a handful, but Sophie insisted. And since she hadn't met Natalya yet, we understood."

"So, she'd met your son, but not your daughter?"

"*Oui*, she came out shortly after Maxim was born."

"To America?"

"*Oui.*"

"I thought you were Russian."

Sergei chuckled. "I am."

"But you live in America, and speak impeccable French."

"*Oui.* I actually speak five languages fluently."

"That's right, I recall Sophie mentioning that. She said it made her feel less homesick while she was in Saint Petersburg to be able to talk to someone who spoke as many languages as her."

"It was entertaining, I will admit, especially since she often switches languages when she's excited or frustrated."

"I don't know about you, but for me, sometimes she sounds like a foreign language convention stuffed into a blender, on its highest setting without the lid on. It just spews out of her in all directions."

"That might be the best description yet." Sergei chuckled and slapped his knee.

"Don't get me wrong, it's one of the many things I love about her, though occasionally it confuses the hell out of me, too."

"Why didn't you join her that year?"

"She was mad at me. And before I knew it, she was spending the year studying abroad."

Sergei's eyes grew wide as he nodded.

"What can I say? When you fall in love with a worldly woman, things get interesting."

"I hope things are better now," Sergei replied.

"Hmm. *Comme ci, comme ça.* Some days are better than others."

"She is a sweet girl."

"*Oui.* And a stubborn mule as well."

Sergei chuckled. "Aren't all women?"

"Too true, my friend. Too true. She exhausts me sometimes. Her impatience will be the end of me, I'm sure."

Sergei shook his head. "*Non.* You have a good woman there. Whatever the problems are, fix them. Don't let her get away. Don't make my mistake."

"I don't understand. Are you not happily married to Addison?"

"*Oui.* But I had to chase her down to get her to marry me. Here in France, in fact. Sophie helped."

"Ah yes, my little matchmaker, always trying to bring people together. I take it Addison was not receptive to the marriage idea."

"Like you said. Stubborn mule."

This had Claude doubled over in laughter. He liked this guy. "*Oui,* that is a woman for you. I have the opposite problem. Sophie wants to get married. Now."

"Lucky man. I wouldn't turn her down if I were you."

"I'm not ready. I need more time." Claude's teeth ground against each other. He really didn't see the problem with waiting a little longer.

Sergei nodded. "I think I understand... just don't take too much time."

Claude tipped his bottle and drained the remaining beer just as Jacques exited the stables. Walking in the shadows, he headed toward the house. Once Jacques reached the foot of the steps, Claude called out to him. "Hey, Jacques, everything okay?"

"Huh? What?" Jacques said.

Claude stood. "Sorry to startle you. We were out here just catching a breath of fresh air. This is Sergei. His family is visiting from America."

"Oh. Of course." Jacques remained standing on the top step.

"While I've got you here, I wanted to let you know that I've talked to *Monsieur* Compte, and we are going to shorten the training schedule for Jezebel for the next week or so."

"Why?" Jacques said.

Claude's eyes narrowed. He hadn't been expecting such a hostile response from the trainer. They pulled horses from the schedule all the time for various issues. It wasn't unusual in the least.

"Nothing serious. She's lost a few pounds and we want to fatten her up a bit. Make sure she's fit. We've changed her diet, so we want to see if that puts her back on track," Claude said.

"I see. Let me know how you would like me to proceed." Jacques' words were terse and clipped.

"Of course."

"Well, goodnight then. I think I'll be heading home." Without another word, Jacques backed down the steps and left them standing on the porch.

"Well, he's strange," Sergei said.

"Caught that, did you? It was odd, indeed."

"Is there a rivalry between the two of you?" Sergei asked.

"No. Not that I know of. But I think he's interested in dating my mother."

"And you are not okay with this?"

"Actually, I have no problem with it at all. Though I don't think he knows that. I was going to say something to that effect tonight, but I didn't get a chance. He seems unusually hostile to me every time I talk to him." Claude shrugged. *There's that feeling again!*

"Interesting," Sergei said. Tipping his bottle back,

he drained it and shook the empty bottle. "I think I could use another beer."

"Interesting, indeed. I agree another beer is in order. Let's get back inside before we are missed."

Claude led the way back through the side door and into the throng of guests milling about. Grabbing two beers from the passing waiter, he maneuvered his way to the back wall they'd been perched against earlier before he passed one to Sergei.

"We've got a long night ahead of us, my friend," Sergei said, and clinked his bottle to Claude's.

"I believe we do." Claude grinned.

CHAPTER 16

Family Dynamics

Sophie

Sophie was enjoying the moment, watching Natalya play on the floor of the library as her parents finished their tea, when Agnes came in. "There's a call for you, Mrs. Petrova. From America."

"That's probably your mother," Sergei said, a mischievous glint in his eye.

"You can take it in the study," Bertrand said.

Addison rolled her eyes at her husband and stood to follow Agnes from the room.

"I hope everything is all right," Sophie said.

"I'm sure it is. Addison's mother can be a bit dramatic." Sergei bounced Maxim on his knee while the little boy continued to stuff teacakes into his already-full mouth.

"Not fond of your mother-in-law?" Bertrand asked.

"Not particularly." Sergei shook his head.

"Which one?" Sophie asked.

"Oh, I love Cassie. And Eli. Tandy, on the other hand, is much harder to get along with."

Bertrand chuckled. "My mother-in-law was a wonderful woman. She took a while to warm up to me, but when she did we were thick as thieves."

Sergei nodded. "That's Cassie, Addison's step-mother. She's not the one who leaves us messages or sends Addison notes that are dipped in a vat of guilt-trip serum."

"Guilt-trip serum." Bertrand laughed. "That would be tough."

"It is. Addison is a grown woman, married with children of her own, but her mother finds it hard to respect boundaries. Any boundaries."

"Ouch," Sophie said as Addison walked back in the room. "Is everything okay?" she asked.

"So, your mother?" Sergei asked.

"Well, it was technically Cassie," Addison said.

"About your mother?" Sergei winked.

"Yes."

"Why is your stepmother calling you in Paris about your mother?" Sophie asked.

"My mom forgot we were going to France apparently, so she was trying to track me down, and called my father, of course."

Sergei started laughing.

Bertrand's brow rose.

Shaking her head, Addison picked up her daughter from the floor where she was scattering stuffed animals around and rested her on her hip. "I need to go call her now. I'll change Nat while I'm on the phone. Want me to take Maxim up and wash him?"

"Nah, I don't think he's done with the cakes yet," Sergei said.

"Don't let him eat too many; he'll get sick." Addison left the room, Natalya chatting away.

Ten minutes later, Agnes came and cleared the tea tray away, upsetting Maxim as he was reaching for another cake.

"I'll just go up and remind Addy that we're going out to dinner tonight," Sophie said.

"Good luck." Sergei chuckled.

Sophie stuck her tongue out at him like a little girl, making Maxim giggle and Sergei laugh harder. The precious sounds carried through the doorway, following her up the stairs. As she walked down the hall, she could hear voices coming from the nursery.

"Say hi to Granny," Addison said.

Natalya's little voice followed. "Grnne."

Sophie smiled. She couldn't wait to be settled down with the little ones. Having Natalya and Maxim here filled her with a joy she could barely contain.

"I don't understand why you spent all that money taking the kids to France. It's not like they're old enough to appreciate it..." a woman's voice whined, her strident tone filling the room. Addison must have the phone on speaker, Sophie realized, as she slipped in through the open doorway.

"It's such a waste..." Addison's mother continued.

Sophie opened her mouth to speak, when Addison glanced up and put her finger to her lips and then pointed to the phone beside her on the changing table.

"Mama, I've got to get ready for dinner. Was there something you needed?"

A loud huff echoed through the phone's speaker. "Do I have to have a reason to want to talk to my daughter?"

Addison lifted her eyes to the ceiling and took a deep breath. "Of course not, Mama, but since I'm calling from Paris I wanted to make sure everything is okay."

"When will you be home so that I can visit my grandchildren? Or is that too much to ask?"

"We'll be home in a couple of weeks. I'll call you when we get home and make plans to have you over for dinner."

"Fine."

"I'll talk to you soon, Mama."

The call disconnected, and Sophie walked over and shut the phone off since Addison had her hands full changing Natalya's diaper.

"Well, that was unpleasant," Sophie said.

"Ugh. You have no idea."

"What was so important that she had to call your father to find you?"

"Apparently, she left three messages on the home phone, and since I hadn't called her back she felt ignored. And God forbid Mama is ever ignored."

Sophie laughed. Reaching into the playpen, she grabbed an overstuffed bird toy covered in feathers and rubbed it against Natalya's cheek, causing her to giggle.

"Seriously, there was no family emergency?"

"Where my mother is concerned, a missed message is."

"I'd forgotten how persistent your mother is..."

Addison shook her head. "She resents the amount of time we spend with my father and Cassie, and feels

slighted if she doesn't get what she feels is her due."
Addison finished changing the baby as Sergei walked in
with Maxim.

"This boy needs a bath," he said as he held Maxim
at arm's length, upside down. Maxim's giggles and
squeals elicited similar sounds from his sister as she
watched him from across the room.

Sergei set Maxim down and kissed Addison's cheek
before heading to their rooms to change. Sophie took
Maxim's hand and led him to the bathroom to
wash up.

"I'm sorry that things are still so strained with your
mother. I would give anything for my *maman* to be
here with us."

"I know you do, and Mama isn't all that bad. She's
just a lot to digest sometimes. Though I do wish she'd
ease up on Sergei a little. At least she's not overtly
hostile anymore."

Sophie nodded. "*Maman* loved Claude. He was
the apple of her eye. She would probably be the one
nagging him to marry me right now."

"Give him time. Some of us just need to feel like
we're in control of our lives a little more before we add
further complications."

"*Merde*, marriage is not a complication."

Addison laughed. "Oh, my friend, but it is. It

really is. You suddenly have to juggle two families, and expectations, and Christmas lists, and work, and home life. And then when you add children, God, it gets even more complicated to keep all the balls in the air instead of crashing to the ground."

"But you are happy?" Sophie asked, suddenly concerned she'd missed something important about her friend's life.

"Oh, blissfully. Don't get me wrong, I love every minute of our hectic life. But it *is* manic sometimes, make no mistake. Life is crazy in any shape or form. At least I'm grateful to have a wonderful partner to share the load."

Sophie kissed the top of Maxim's head. "Come, let us get dressed and go out and show the children the town."

Addison had given her some food for thought. It was similar to what her father had said about life before she'd been born. Sophie craved what they had, but took their words to heart.

CHAPTER 17

A Fine Mess

Sophie

Shouting drew Sophie out of the stables, where she'd been showing off the horses to Addison and Sergei.

Her father stood across the paddock squared off with none other than *Monsieur* Martin, their family's longest friend, and the stables' biggest client. Her father's hands were tightly fisted, his face beet-red. As she came up beside her father, she placed a hand on his arm. His muscles clenched beneath her fingers. Claude reached the paddock where they stood, moments later.

"Papa?"

Bertrand never took his eyes from *Monsieur* Martin as he patted her hand. "How dare you!"

Monsieur Martin shrugged. "I'm just telling you what the Ministry told me. Balthazar tested positive this morning."

Sophie choked on the air she inhaled, coughing and sputtering as her father continued to yell at *Monsieur* Martin.

"You accuse me of cheating and drugging my horse. *Non*, I'll not stand for it."

"*My* horse," *Monsieur* Martin responded.

"*Humph*!" Bertrand continued to glare daggers at *Monsieur* Martin.

"It was an honest assessment." *Monsieur* Martin shrugged.

"How do we know the doping happened here and not at your stables?" Bertrand shouted.

"That's ridiculous." *Monsieur* Martin said, his voice rising again.

"How dare you come here accusing me, and don't even consider it could happen at your stables instead of here." Bertrand's voice continued to rise.

"Then test all the horses here." *Monsieur* Martin suggested.

"Surely you can't be serious!" Claude gasped.

Bertrand glared at their longest and most loyal customer as though he was a stranger.

"Don't be a stubborn fool," *Monsieur* Martin said, his shoulders stiffening.

Sophie gasped. They had never been accused of something so nefarious before.

"*Non*, we will test them all, on the condition that you test your stables as well," Bertrand relented.

Monsieur Martin nodded.

"Call Doc Stratford and ask him to come at once," Bertrand said.

"But Papa, Claude and I can do the testing," Sophie said. Their stables would never survive the scandal of having all of their horses tested for doping. The mere accusation alone, once it reached the public, would be enough to tarnish her family's reputation forever. It would be best to keep it as quiet as they could.

Bertrand patted her hand again. "I know, *ma chère fille. Non.* We'll have Dr. Stratford do it to show we have nothing to hide."

Monsieur Martin said, "Thank you for taking this seriously."

"*Humph*! How could I not?" Bertrand asked.

"So, you'll be returning Balthazar to us then?" Sophie directed her question to *Monsieur* Martin.

"*Non. Sur mon cadavre*," *Monsieur* Martin said, followed by a string of expletives. His face flushed as his voice rose another octave. The vein in his forehead throbbed with his words.

"Then a reimbursement for your troubles?" she asked.

"*Oui,* that would be fair."

"Okay, then, we will get a check out to you in the morning. Will that work?" Sophie asked.

"*Oui,* and the test results—you will share those with me, correct?"

Sophie bit her lip as her father's body stiffened beside her. A quick glance down showed that his fists had still not unclenched. She had little doubt that if *Monsieur* Martin, loyal, long-standing customer or not, did not leave, her father was bound to punch him in the nose at some point for what he no doubt perceived as continued insults.

"Of course," Claude said. "And you will share yours?"

"*Oui.*" Taking a deep breath, *Monsieur* Martin shoved his hand out toward Claude, who shook it.

"Well, then, I look forward to hearing from you." With a brisk nod, *Monsieur* Martin returned to his car parked at the edge of the paddock and drove away.

Sophie let out the breath she'd been holding as she searched Claude's face. His eyes were wide, and his face had drained of all color. Her stomach roiled as nausea set in. This was surreal. Her eyelid began to twitch, and her hands trembled as she stuffed them into her jacket pockets.

Movement behind him, back toward the barn, caught her attention. Glancing that way, she watched as their stable manager, Eddie, quickly backtracked, moving out of sight. He hadn't joined the rest of the staff who had rushed out during the commotion. That was unlike him.

What's with Eddie?

How weird. Shaking her head, she didn't have time to concern herself with Eddie's odd behavior at the moment, but she would certainly be looking for him later. As she turned her attention back to the staff surrounding them, people began talking over each other.

"*Monsieur* Compte, Ms. Sophie, what does this all mean?" Jean, the stable boy, asked.

After a moment, when she realized her father wasn't going to speak, she said, "I'm not sure." She leaned in to her father. Worry filled her as she took in his stiff posture and beet-red face.

Jean turned to Claude, who shrugged.

"Come, Papa, let us go back to the house and sit down for a moment. Let us catch our breath and get a drink. We can discuss things more clearly then."

Bertrand nodded.

"Ms. Sophie?" Jean interrupted.

"*Je m'excuse.* Everyone, please excuse us while we try to figure things out."

With that, the staff that had gathered around them returned to their duties as Sophie walked with her father and Claude back to the main house.

Climbing the steps, she gave Marte a small nod as she stood wringing her hands on the porch. Addison and her husband stood slightly off to the side, against the railing, their eyes wide and their bodies tense. In the background, the sounds of the children playing in the house filtered out through the open door.

―――――――

Sophie heaved the file she was reading off her desk. *Fils de pute!* She spit out the expletive as the file hit the floor with an ominous thud. The morning wasn't starting out any better than the previous day had ended.

Shortly after their council of war over stiff drinks in the sitting room, Claude had reached out and asked the on-call veterinarian, Dr. Stratford, to come out immediately. Under the circumstances, he agreed time was of the essence. Dr. Stratford had been the veteri-

narian of choice for the Compte stables for more than
a decade as Claude and Sophie studied.

Unfortunately, the results were less than satisfac-
tory. In fact, her father was in such a state of shock that
she had convinced him to visit his cardiologist in town
instead of coming to the farm today.

Pushing her chair back, she leaned down and
picked the doctor's report off of the floor and dropped
it back on her desk. There was no point in trying to
hide from it, as much as the fight-or-flight instinct
inside her wished she could. The reality was that,
somehow, their life's work was about to be ruined.
And for the life of her, she couldn't understand who
was responsible or why.

The farm and the family's reputation had always
been second to none. They had no reason to cheat. It
served no purpose for them. Yet the results were in. Dr.
Stratford had checked everything twice, agreeing that,
having never had a previous history or accusation of
unethical behavior, it was paramount to check everything again. No one wanted to make a mistake now.
Too much hung in the balance.

How the hell are we going to fix this?

Overnight, her family's whole world had been
upended. They had dozens of people depending on
them, and yet all she could think about was the way

her father looked this morning at breakfast. She'd sent him to his doctor and Addison and Sergei on a day of sightseeing so that she could come to the stables and work with Claude on how they could mitigate the disaster.

Glancing down at the file on her desk she scanned down the page, with the test results showing the levels of the various drugs in the horses' systems. She ignored the numbers. They hadn't changed in the four times she'd read it before, so her eyes traveled further down the page to the bottom where the summary of the report was.

Examination's findings: Blood tests revealed high levels of a recombinant form of hGH called somatropin, a synthetic growth hormone, and recombinant human erythropoietin (rhEPO), causing increased blood viscosity which can enhance their endurance capacity. These results were found in Jezebel, Twilight, and Morningstar, and four colts, Magnus and Zorro, Saragon, and Tornado.

There is no medical reason for a horse to be treated with these substances, and the high levels in such young animals is concerning.

Well, no kidding. Of course, there was no medical reason for the horses to have any of these drugs in their system. Compte Stables was a breeding farm, not a racing stable. There was no purpose to push the horses that were to be sold to outside racing stables.

Damn it all to hell. It was interesting, though, that only the horses in the main stables had been affected. Goliath, the youngest colt, had just been weaned and moved over from the paddock and so had not been drugged. So, it looked like only those old enough to be broken and trained were at risk.

With a huff, she slammed the folder shut. This didn't make any sense.

Claude poked his head in through the doorway. "*Ma chérie,* do not fret. We will fix this."

"*Comment?*"

"I suggest we hire a private investigator to do background checks."

"Our staff is beyond reproach," she said.

"*Oui,* and our horses were always clean." Claude's lips pursed. "Until now."

"*Touché.*" She loved the way he said 'our'. It made her feel less alone in this battle.

"So, I suggest starting at the beginning. If nothing else, it will clear us."

"Clear us?"

"Sophie, *mon amour*, we have been the on-staff veterinarians here as part of our internship. Who do you think will be the first to be accused? The doctors, of course."

Merde! That thought had actually never even crossed her mind. Not only would her family's business be destroyed, but any medical future for her or Claude would be as well.

"When I get my hands on who did this..." she muttered.

"*Oui, mon coeur,* but first we must find them. Then we can mangle them. Together."

"I like the sound of that. Okay, a private investigator, but we must keep this to ourselves. The staff would not understand. They would feel slighted." Sophie sighed.

"I will make some calls."

"*S'il vous plait.* I need to call *Monsieur* Martin to discuss his next steps."

"Do you think he'll sue?" Claude asked. He walked over and put his arms around her.

Resting her head on his chest, she said, "Honestly, I'm more concerned about him going public, period!"

"I'll get started right away. Meet for lunch at the house?"

"I have no appetite," Sophie said.

"We need to keep up appearances and go through

the motions, if for nothing else than the staff. They must see us strong."

Sophie nodded. "I'll see you at the house at noon."

Claude leaned down and kissed the top of her head. Sophie leaned up and caught his lips as he lifted his head. He lowered his lips and kissed her again before heading out of the office, leaving her alone once again.

With a heavy heart and a long sigh, she picked up her phone to call *Monsieur* Martin.

CHAPTER 18
Friends or Foes

Claude

Claude decided to make the calls from his mother's house. He figured the chances of being overheard in his office were too high. The staff was a tightknit group of people, closer than family. Not only was the future of Compte Stables at stake, but their livelihoods were as well. There was also the fact that they had a traitor in their midst. Whether or not Sophie or Bertrand realized that, there was no room for doubt where he was concerned. This was not an accident that happened. This was methodical. This took time, and in his opinion there was just no way a stranger who did not belong would have had the access necessary to drug as many of the horses that they now knew were involved. Someone would have noticed. The test results showed that the horses had to have been dosed on more than one occasion.

It turned his stomach to think that someone had been harming the horses for so long, right under his nose. He had never suspected that Jezebel's weight loss was due to a reaction to the drugs, not simply a dietary need.

They could only hope that, now that they knew, they could prevent further actions against the horses.

He pulled out the old phone book his mother always kept a copy of and started looking through the pages for private investigators. He didn't dare risk using the computer right now. A search history would be too obvious and would tip their hand. Claude didn't know who they could trust, so it was better to trust no one. Except for Sophie, of course. Her world was just as tied up in this as his. She stood to lose everything. And it wasn't in her nature to cheat. For any reason.

Flipping through the pages, he found a full-page ad that caught his eye.

CORPORATE SERVICES
New employee background checks:

- *Job History Verification*
- *Credit History Search*
- *Criminal History Search*

Know who they are before you hire them.

This was perfect. While there weren't many new employees, someone at the stables had to be responsible. And since most had been with the Compte family for years, if not decades, no one would suspect them, and *Monsieur* Compte hadn't done thorough background checks before any of the older staff were hired.

Claude dialed the number at the top of the page, and after three rings it went to voicemail. He left his name and his mobile number, not giving too much information, just a request for a callback.

As he was disconnecting, the screen door thumped as it closed and his mother walked into the kitchen, followed by Jacques.

He slammed the phonebook closed, earning him a side look from his mother.

"Everything okay?" she asked.

"*Oui.* Just looking up some information."

"Need any help?" she asked.

"*Non.* I've got it covered."

"Has *Monsieur* Compte figured out who doped the horses yet?" Jacques asked.

Claude looked at him leaning against the door-frame. He had not come fully into the room, instead stood just on the perimeter. There was an aloofness to him that rubbed Claude the wrong way. He still couldn't put his finger on it. Maybe he *was* jealous of his mother's new relationship, after all, and he just couldn't admit it. Jacques had been nothing but cordial around him. So there really was no excuse to dislike him. He really wanted his mother to find happiness for herself after all this time. There was just something about Jacques. And it bothered him. Deeply.

"*Non*. He is not at the farm today."

"Where is he?" Jacques asked.

"Doctor's."

"Oh, I see," Jacques replied.

"Would you like to stay for lunch?" Leila asked.

Claude stood. "I can't today, I'm meeting Sophie at the house for lunch. Care to join us?"

"*Non*," Jacques said quickly.

His mother arched a brow at Jacques' hasty reply but didn't comment. "Go, have lunch with Sophie. She could use your support. Give her my love."

"Thanks, *Maman*," Claude said. He leaned in and gave his mother a kiss on the cheek, and with a short nod at Jacques he left the kitchen.

Walking briskly to the main house, he mulled over

the last few times he'd had run-ins with Jacques. There was a niggling in his gut, but he couldn't place it.

"*Bonjour*, Claude, how are you today?" Marte asked.

"*Stressé!*"

Marte nodded as she continued to make her way to the kitchen.

Claude followed her. They only ate in the dining room when Bertrand was present. Sophie preferred the comfort of the kitchen, surrounded by the bustling of Carson and Marte.

She was already seated at the big center island, laughing at something he'd missed. Her face was flushed, and her eyes danced. It was good to see her happy, even if it was just for a moment.

She gave him a bright smile as he sat down beside her. His breath caught in his throat. They were in this together. No matter where the cards fell, they would stand by one another.

"Did you make the call?" she asked.

He narrowed his eyes and shook his head. She bit her lip and nodded.

"What call? Is everything all right?" Marte asked.

"It's fine, we were just going to call to check on Bertrand. I thought we should do it after lunch, together," Claude said.

"*Oui,* we are all worried," Marte said.

"Please ask him if there is anything we can do when you talk to him," Carson added.

"Of course," Sophie said.

Marte served them up a hearty stew and then began tidying up the kitchen. "Are the children going to visit today?" she asked.

"*Non.* Today they are tourists in the city."

"Maybe tomorrow?" Marte asked hopefully.

Claude exchanged a look with Sophie.

"*Oui,* maybe tomorrow," Sophie said.

Lunch was over quickly, and after kissing Marte's and Carson's cheeks Sophie led him out of the house.

"Are you up for a walk?" he asked.

"*Oui.*" She tucked her hands into his crooked elbow.

"I left a message for a private investigator. I hope to hear back shortly."

"That is good, but why did you not want to talk in front of Marte and Carson? We can trust them."

"*Non.* At this moment we cannot trust anyone," he said.

"Claude!"

"I'm serious. Talk to no one. Trust no one but your father."

Sophie stopped short. "I trust you," she said.

"And I you. We are as one. But we have a traitor that we must flush out, and even though most of the staff is innocent you never know where a careless word might reach. The less everyone else knows, the better." He tugged her arm and she started walking again.

"I can't believe that it would be one of us."

"Honestly, it could be none other," he said. "We don't often have strangers roaming around. That would have been noticed, and sparked talk."

"Where should we start?" she asked.

"Everywhere. With everyone."

"Seriously?"

"*Oui,* including you and me, and your father." Claude's gaze bored into her.

"Not Papa!" Sophie's eye twitched.

"*Oui,* everyone. It is as much to clear us of suspicion as it is to find the culprit."

"God, this is all so sordid." Sophie shuddered.

"It must be done. It would serve no purpose to do a partial job."

"I understand. I don't like it, not for one moment. But I agree," she said.

He pulled her closer. "*Je t'aime.*"

"And I you," she said.

"I'll let you know what the investigator says once I talk to them."

157

"I'll need to go with you when you meet up."

"Why?" Claude stopped and stared at her.

"Because I'll need to pay for it from my private account."

"*Oui*, of course. I didn't think."

Sophie shrugged. "I figured it wouldn't be wise to use the business account if we aren't sure who we can trust."

"Smart girl. That's why I love you."

"Come to dinner tonight at the apartment?"

"I would like that." Claude wrapped his arms around her, pulling her close for a deep kiss. "I'll see you tonight."

He released her and headed back to the stables. He wanted to check on the horses again. With what was going on, he would be spending even more time with them. They needed to get to the bottom of not only who was drugging the horses, and of course why, but the most important aspect he needed to focus on was how. How had this happened right under their noses?

CHAPTER 19

Disturbing Trends

Sophie

"Papa?" Sophie called out, reaching the door of his study. The light was on, but he wasn't behind his desk like she had expected him to be.

"*Mademoiselle*, he's in the drawing room," Agnes said.

"*Merci*."

"The Petrovas have returned as well."

"That's great. Claude will be joining us for dinner."

"Of course, *Mademoiselle*."

Sophie nodded and made her way into the drawing room. Sergei was sitting on the floor with the kids, playing with an enormous caboose to a train set. Little Maxim sat across from him— wide, adoring eyes staring at the train car.

Her father's skin looked a little less pasty this evening. Then again, he had a brandy in his hand, which may have accounted for the color in his cheeks.

"Papa, how did the appointment with your doctor go?"

"Fine. I'm fine," Bertrand said.

She walked over and kissed his cheek before heading over to pour herself a drink. She preferred a vodka martini to the heavier alcohols her father enjoyed. Once her martini was mixed, she joined Addison on the lounge to catch up on the day's adventures.

A few moments later, Claude arrived.

"Ah, good of you to join us, my boy," Bertrand said.

"We should put the children to bed before we eat," Addison suggested.

"*Oui*," Sergei agreed. "Come, Maxim, let's pick up your train and kiss everyone goodnight."

"Keesses!" Maxim cried. He stood up, wobbled, and after righting himself bee-lined directly to Sophie.

"They are not joining us?" she asked.

"The kids have already had their supper," Sergei said.

"Well, then, kisses for you." Sophie set her glass down on the table and picked up the squirming little boy. He wrapped his arms around her neck and placed a sloppy kiss on her lips.

"Ponieez man!" Maxim said.

Claude leaned in and kissed his cheek. "Sleep tight, tiger. We'll see you soon."

Maxim bobbed his head in response.

Sergei reached out and took him from Sophie. "Finish your drink. We will be back down shortly."

Addison retrieved the sleeping Natalya from her rocking seat and followed Sergei out of the room.

Claude poured himself a brandy and then took the seat vacated by Addison. "Sir, are you well enough for an update?" he asked.

Bertrand rolled his eyes to the ceiling. "Stop fussing. You sound just as bad as her." He pointed the glass in his hand at Sophie, who grinned and shrugged in response. "Tell me what you've learned."

"I've learned nothing yet, sir. However, I did reach out to a private investigating firm and left a message for them. I suggested to Sophie that we have them run background checks on everyone. Including us."

Bertrand nodded. "Good thinking."

"And Sophie suggested we pay for their services with her private card, and not through the stables' accounts."

Bertrand glanced at Sophie. "Another fine idea. Where do we go from here?"

"Well, sir, once we get the firm started on the background checks, we should run an internal audit on the books. To see if there are any more discrepancies."

Bertrand's eyes narrowed. "Explain."

"Well, there are some additional costs in the general ledger that don't make sense. We've been spending far more than usual, and there is no notation as to why," Claude said.

"*Merde!*" Bertrand said. "I forgot all about that."

"About what, Papa?"

"Before you took over the accounting, our longtime leather vendor closed up shop. I decided to give a local boy the business. He's young and a little more expensive than what we've paid in the past, but I'm satisfied with his products so far."

"Ah, well, that explains the ledgers. Good to know."

"Finish telling me about the audit," Bertrand said.

"Well, to be honest, I can't for the life of me understand the motive. It has to be money."

"*Oui,* drugging the horses does no one any good if

the horses are being sold to others, not raced for ourselves."

"Exactly, sir. Why drug the horses that are being sold? It might blemish your reputation as a breeder, but only if it is discovered right away. But again, these horses were already sold, almost from birth. So why these horses? They were all going to different buyers. The sales were common knowledge around the farm."

"So, what are you suggesting?" Sophie asked.

"I'm wondering if maybe this is a decoy or a diversion of some sort."

"For what purpose?"

"To hide a different crime. I just don't know."

"Who would do this to us? Haven't we always been a generous employer?" Bertrand asked. He took a gulp of his drink, draining his glass.

"Papa, you have always been a good and generous man. Don't fret. We will find the truth."

"Sophie, darling. The truth is already apparent."

"Papa?"

"Someone has betrayed us. Someone we trust."

Sophie hung her head. Just as Claude had suggested earlier in the day, as much as she hated it, it had become her fear as well. How did one recover from such a betrayal from within? And how did they stop it before whoever was responsible did further damage?

She glanced up at Claude. At least they were working together on this.

"We will hire the firm and review the books starting in the morning. Come, let us have a nice family dinner and put these worries aside for tonight," Bertrand said.

Sophie nodded. The whole situation was over-whelming. Her parents had worked so hard to build the business into what it was today, a world-renowned breeding farm. And suddenly everything they had hung in the balance. It wasn't the money she cared about, or even their personal reputations that really mattered at the end of the day. It was their family. They had hundreds of people who worked for them, depended on them, and would be hurt if they couldn't save the farm. The very idea of letting them down haunted her even more than the heartbreak her father would face.

Sophie set her martini down and stood, following the men into the dining room just as Sergei and Addison returned.

CHAPTER 20

Frustration Peaks

Claude

Claude returned to the stables after dinner, not wanting to be far from the horses. Sophie had not been pleased. She had expected him to stay the night. Why couldn't she understand? Their future was at stake.

He stopped by the stables first. Jezebel was restless again and, if he didn't know better, spooked. She head-bumped the door to her stall, rattling it against the lock.

"Hey, pretty girl," he crooned, stroking her muzzle.

He opened his palm, exposing an apple slice. She bumped the hand stroking her before she stretched her neck and snatched the apple.

"There you go. Better now?" he asked.

He stroked her neck as she chomped on her treat. It soothed him to be near her. The drugs would be out of her system soon, and he'd make damn sure she was never drugged again. God help the bastard if he caught him.

"Claude, is everything okay?" Eddie asked.

He turned just as Eddie lumbered up to him. "*Oui*, just giving Jezebel a late-night snack. And you?"

"Just making my rounds before bed."

"Good job. Anything new?"

"No, sir. Just feel responsible."

"Why is that?" Claude asked.

"They are such beautiful souls. For them to be harmed on our watch just feels wrong." Heat crept up his neck and his stomach tightened.

Determined, Claude would put people he trusted on twenty-four-hour watch if that was what it took. "I know how you feel. We'll keep a better watch on them from now on."

"*Oui*. They will not be harmed again. That I can promise you and *Monsieur* Bertrand."

Claude patted Jezebel's neck one last time and then pushed away from her stall. "Walk with me. We'll give the rest of them their treats together. Then we can head off to bed." Though he considered making his bed right here in the stables.

"Yes, sir." Eddie accepted the apple slices that Claude pulled from his pocket and beamed at him.

Twenty minutes later, the horses in the stable all had an apple to chomp on and Claude felt satisfied that they were safe for the night. He couldn't know for sure, but his gut told him they wouldn't have another issue right away.

Two days had passed since they'd hired the private investigator to do the background checks, and they still were no closer to learning the truth. Addison and Sergei had offered to help and, seeing as they were respected by Bertrand and had nothing to gain by harming the horses, Bertrand had them going through the financial accounts. They were looking for discrepancies compared to the previous five years while Sophie searched the stables' orders and supply logs for the same period. If they didn't find anything they would call in an expert, but for now Sophie was sure they could figure this out internally. Maxim and Natalya were in the house with Carson and Marte, baking chocolate chip cookies.

After rapping on the glass with his knuckles, he opened the door to Sophie's office. Sergei and Addison were huddled at the spare desk in the corner, while Sophie faced her computer, her bottom lip between her teeth.

"*Bonjour.*" He stepped inside the office and shut the door with a click.

She looked up. "Lunch?"

"*Oui,* figured you might need a reminder." He grinned.

Sophie punched a few buttons on her keyboard and, with a couple clicks of her mouse, shut down her computer.

Sergei and Addison closed the files spread out in front of them and stacked them in the corner of the desk. Sergei helped his wife out of her chair and then filed out as Claude held the door open for them. Turning, Sophie locked the door behind her with a sigh.

"It won't be long, *ma chérie.*"

He wrapped his arm around her shoulder and pulled her close. It hurt his heart to see her so defeated, so lost. Her whole world had changed in an instant and it would never be the same for her. Their small group walked to the house in silence. Frustration sat heavy on his soul.

Maxim came barreling down the steps, passing

Marte on the porch. "Papa!" he squealed. Sergei picked him up and tossed him in the air before settling him on his hip.

Addison climbed the steps and reached for Natalya, who was squirming in Marte's outstretched arms.

"Ah, there you are. How were they this morning, Marte?"

"Angels as always," Marte said.

"Hmm. She must be talking about someone else's kids," Addison said to the wiggling bundle in her arms.

"Definitely not talking about our two monsters," Sergei agreed.

"Monsers!" Maxim agreed, bobbing his head.

This eased the tension they had been feeling as they left Sophie's office, and everyone laughed.

Marte winked at them as she held the door open.

Bertrand was already in the dining room when they filed in.

"I hope you don't mind, but I thought we'd have the children eat with us today. I thought we could use some cheering up."

"Oh boy," Addison said. "It must be really bad if he wants a messy dining room and two mess-making children to join us."

Bertrand chuckled. "Enjoy this time with them.

They grow up fast. Too fast." He glanced over at Sophie.

Sophie blushed as she kissed her father's cheek before she took her seat to the left of him. His stomach rolled as he noticed that the laughter hadn't reached Bertrand's eyes. He was tense again. Something had changed from their last conversation. It was written all over his face.

Claude took his seat across from her, on Bertrand's right, while the children were put into old-fashioned high chairs between their parents.

Having Maxim and Natalya in the room made things livelier, but they were a distraction that made it impossible to talk about the status of the investigation. Claude sat to the side, uncomfortable during the meal though he wasn't sure why. There was this feeling in his gut that things were going to get much worse before they got better.

CHAPTER 21

Bubbling to the Surface

Sophie

Sophie grinned as the kids made a mess of their meals. Lunch was short but entertaining, and at least everyone was more relaxed than they had been in days. Marte came in and snatched up Maxim, while Addison carried Natalya into the kitchen behind her.

"The detectives delivered their initial report this morning," Bertrand said.

"What did they find, Papa?" Sophie asked.

"I'll be honest, the report was unexpected."

"Tell us, Papa. Who did this to us?" Sophie pushed her plate away.

"The most interesting thing is here." Bertrand

171

tapped the stack of papers. "It says there are 275,000 euros in your account," he said, looking directly at Claude.

"*Merde!*" Claude sucked in his breath in an audible hiss.

"Where did it come from?" Bertrand asked.

The blood drained from his face. "You can't really think I would betray you—"

"Papa, he wouldn't," Sophie cried.

"Follow the money. It's there in black and white." Bertrand tapped the report in his hand.

"How dare you!" Claude hollered as he jumped out of his chair, letting it crash to the floor as he stormed out.

Carson, Marte, and Addison came rushing into the room as the screen door slammed.

"What happened?" Addison asked.

Sophie remained mute as she glared at her father.

"Apparently, there is an exceptionally large sum of money in Claude's bank account," Sergei explained.

"Oh, Sophie," Addison cried.

Marte gasped. Turning, she ushered Carson from the room.

"Papa, how could you think..." Sophie whispered.

"I don't."

Startled, Sophie paused. "Then why—"

"The money is in his account."

"You just said you didn't believe he would betray you. Us."

"I don't."

"But—"

"*Ma chèrie,* stop and consider. The money is in his account. How did it get there? Think, girl. Use the brain God gave you."

"You think that the traitor is not just close to the farm, but close to Claude himself," Sergei suggested.

Bertrand lifted his glass in a mock salute. "Bingo. Someone went to great lengths to make Claude look guilty in order to divert the attention away from him or herself."

"But his account?" Sophie asked.

"I imagine that information would be easy to get from his bedroom. His bank book is probably in his desk at home."

Addison's eyes grew wide as she continued to stand in the doorway. "But certainly Claude would have known about the money."

"According to the report, it was an electronic transfer from a Cayman Islands account yesterday. It had been flagged, which is why Claude might not have seen it."

"Oh, Papa, what do we do now?"

"We let everyone think we believe Claude is the culprit for now, so they let their guard down."

"I must tell him."

"No! God, no. Someone close to us did this. Someone who may have a grudge against him we do not know about. We need Claude to think we believe he might have done this, so he will act accordingly for now."

"The investigators will continue to search for the real criminal, though, right? You're not giving up on him, are you?" Sophie begged.

"Of course not. We'll find the truth. And we will set things right with Claude. I promise."

The mood was dampened as they returned to her office to continue poring over the accounts. Sergei and Addison left early to take the children home, while she worked a little longer. Her stomach sour and her mind distracted, she couldn't help but think she would miss something being so concerned about Claude.

At the end of the day when she drove past his mother's house, the lights were out and the house was closed up tight. Neither car was in front. Her heart broke for them. They were family and they had just been shunned.

They had to figure this out soon.

Sophie had not seen or heard from Claude since he'd stormed out the day before. The silent treatment was common when they were at odds with each other. Her heart ached for him. It was killing her that he thought they didn't trust him. The phone rang on her desk, yanking her from her befuddled state.

"*Bonjour,*" she said.

"Balthazar sired a foal before you sold him to me," *Monsieur* Martin said in response.

"*Oui,* Magnus is his colt. We always sire one breeding from the horses. You know this."

"*Non,* not him."

"Pardon?"

"There is a colt called Wanderlust" *Monsieur* Martin said.

"*Merde!* Who tells you such nonsense?" Sophie swallowed the bile rising in her throat. Her stomach rioted as the morning's coffee threatened to expel itself violently.

"I just received a press release of new horses expected to appear in the Dubai races next season."

"Dubai? Not France?"

"I keep track of international races to see who a contender might be here."

"I see. I never knew. There must be some mistake. Balthazar only sired Magnus. That's the only time he's stood at stud."

"The press release says Wanderlust was sired by Balthazar of Compte Stables in France, and Lady Chatterley of St. Croix Farms in Brazil."

"Brazil? I don't understand. We haven't bred a non-European horse ever before. That's not who we are," Sophie said.

"Well, I'm looking at it in black and white."

"Who does it claim is Lady Chatterley's sire?"

There was a brief pause before *Monsieur* Martin responded. "El Diablo of El Dorado Stables also in Brazil."

She closed her eyes and dropped her head to the desk, the phone still to her ear. This was far worse than she could have imagined. Could someone have altered the official breeding records?

"*Monsieur* Martin, I do not know who would perpetrate such a fabrication. Or why. All I can say is that Balthazar has always been in our control, has never left France, and the only colt he has sired is Magnus. And there have not been any foreign horses on-site ever."

"I'd say it looks like your left hand doesn't know what your right hand is doing, to start with. And I'd certainly say that the exclusivity we have come to expect from your stables is no longer what it used to be."

Sophie let out a strangled moan. "*Monsieur* Martin, you know not what you say."

"But I do, girl. I do. This is a travesty of the highest order."

"Sir, *s'excuser*. I don't know what else to say. This isn't how we do business." She opened her eyes again but lacked the energy to raise her head.

"I wish I could believe that. There is something fishy going on at your farm."

"I agree. We are looking into it."

"I certainly hope so, *Mademoiselle*."

"Please understand we have no cause to deceive you. Give us a chance to get to the bottom of this. Can you give us more time before you go public about the drugs?" Sophie asked.

"Public?" *Monsieur* Martin hissed. "It is not my habit to air other's dirty laundry in public."

"*Merci beaucoup.*"

"*Mademoiselle* Compte, may I offer you a piece of advice?"

"Of course, sir."

"Get your affairs in order. You need to clean house before someone burns it to the ground,"

Monsieur Martin said. His tone clipped leaving no doubt

"I agree, sir. Just bear with us. Your patronage means the world to us."

"We shall talk soon."

"*Au revoir.*"

Her face still plastered to her desk, she dropped the phone back into the cradle. Not one to make a habit of swearing, the words escaped in her frustration. "*Brûle en l'enfer!*" she screamed.

She was emotionally and physically drained. Whoever had it out for them had certainly attacked from multiple different avenues, in a way that they had never suspected. Taking a deep breath, she closed her eyes again and began to cry. Her entire body shook from the force of her sobs.

CHAPTER 22

When All Else Fails

Claude

Claude sat on the back patio of a longtime friend of his parents, staring at the pond. His mother continued to cry herself to sleep at night. It broke his heart how her world had been turned inside out. He had hoped to protect her, to provide for her, and suddenly it was because of him that she'd lost everything. Emotionally gutted, he'd packed his bags and he and his mother had left the Compte property right after his fateful lunch three days ago.

I've lost everything. The love of my life. My career. My future. No matter what they've always said, I was only the hired help.

How could Sophie believe him capable of such deception? He couldn't wrap his head around any of it. To betray them would be a bad enough accusation, but the idea that he could be responsible for bringing harm to the horses was unfathomable. He thought he knew her, but clearly she was easily swayed to believe the worst of him.

He couldn't sleep, his stomach roiled with nausea, his appetite had left him, and his head throbbed. He hadn't felt this ill in years. He continued to reach for his mobile, a part of him itching to call or text Sophie, but he couldn't bring himself to turn the phone back on.

"Would you like some lemonade?" Leila asked.

"*Merci.*" Claude nodded.

"Have you talked to Sophie?"

"*Non.*"

"Please don't let your pride come between you and Sophie. Whatever else happens."

"*Maman,* it's not that simple." He hung his head. Shame filled him.

"You must let me call Bertrand. Surely they can be made to see reason."

"*Non, Maman.* Don't bother."

"Jacques doesn't believe that."

"You've spoken to him?" Claude could barely contain his surprise at this information.

"*Oui,* he called me the morning after we left. Told me that everyone is subdued. But that no one believes you guilty, that Bertrand must have made a mistake."

Claude shook his head. He was defeated. He never expected Sophie and her father would question his loyalty. Whoever had done this would get away with it if Bertrand and Sophie didn't continue digging for the truth. But as far as he was concerned, there was nothing more he could do now that he was on the outside looking in. He needed to figure out a new future for himself and his mother. They couldn't rely on the generosity of friends forever.

"We must sort it all out. I want to go home."

"Oh, *Maman.* I wish I had your unshakable faith. We're homeless. Ostracized from our friends and life. This was not how I imagined the start of my life, after university, to go. I'm not even sure that I'll be allowed to remain a veterinarian when everyone hears of this."

"Jacques said it hasn't gone public. That somehow Sophie and Bertrand have managed to keep it all in-house. Only Dr. Stratford and *Monsieur* Martin know anything."

"That is good. Maybe they will contain it before it

consumes them. I pray that they don't lose everything."

"We will land on our feet, Claude. Our family always has, just as when we lost your papa."

"*Oui,* we will survive." *Somehow.* Claude sipped his lemonade in silence and wondered if maybe he should look into teaching at the veterinary college. The fear of losing the veterinary license, he had only just received, because of the drugged horses had his mind spinning. He had the knowledge and the experience, and if he couldn't be a vet anymore maybe he could teach those who would be. He would reach out to his professors in the morning and see if they had any suggestions.

His mind whirled with the ramifications, over-whelmed. There was a feeling of finality to it all, like experiencing a death in the family. It certainly was the end of his relationship with Sophie and his career at the farm.

He closed his eyes as the bitterness of the lemonade settled into his already-sour stomach.

"Maybe we should drive out to the farm and talk to Jacques. He might be able to help."

"*Maman,* no one can help us now."

"I don't believe that for a minute. You must fight. You must not surrender so easily. Come on. We can drive out there and talk to him."

"Why don't you call him?"

"I've tried, but he hasn't responded for the last two days. I'm worried. It's not like him not to answer my calls."

Alarm bells rang in his ears. There was something not right with the idea that Jacques had gone quiet. It didn't sit well with him.

CHAPTER 23

The Abyss

Sophie

S ophie knew that she was going against her father's orders. She couldn't help herself. Claude had to know she didn't believe any of it. They would get to the truth. She couldn't stop until they did.

Her bottom lip was tucked between her teeth as she texted him.

Claude, we must talk.

No response.

Looking at the screen the other texts all lined up, all from her to him with no reply. There hadn't been a single response to any of her calls or texts in the last three days. She had no idea where he'd gone. She should have gone to him after her father had dropped the bomb on them at lunch. The shock of it all had rooted her feet to the ground. Torn between following her heart and obeying her father's wishes, she'd watched him storm from the house and out of her life without saying a word. She would spend the rest of their lives together making it up to him, as soon as she could convince him to talk to her.

She pounded her fists on the desk. The deposit had led nowhere. Even the bank couldn't clarify the real origin of the money, only that it had been routed through three foreign accounts before reaching Claude's. *Another dead end. Damn it!*

After much persuasion her father had agreed to go home for the day, taking the children with him after dinner. Sergei and Addison had stayed behind with her to continue working on the files, trying to make sense of everything. Not that it was doing them a damn bit of good.

Every day seemed to get worse. The hits kept coming. First, their horses were drugged. Then the obscene deposit into Claude's account. Then, Claude and Leila left the farm and disappeared. He wasn't returning her calls or texts. Now this strange new horse, Wanderlust, somehow sired by their Balthazar.

The detectives were looking into that horse's actual

lineage to see if it was legitimate, though they couldn't account for how it was possible. Nothing made sense anymore. She needed to talk to Claude. Damn him. He had to know her better than this. To know she would never believe such a thing of him.

As she glanced at the clock on the wall, the hands hovering at the eight-thirty position, the air escaped her lungs in a rush. Her chest was tight as the tears welled in her eyes. She was exhausted. The room was closing in on her. This was an experience she wished she could skip. They were nowhere near figuring out what was really going on. The frustration welling up inside her pushed her to the limits. She was beginning to lose hope that things would ever be right again. At this point, if the truth hit them in the face they'd probably miss it.

Inhaling a shaky breath, she shut the file she had been staring uncomprehendingly at for the last twenty minutes. This wasn't getting her anywhere. After pushing her chair back from the desk, she stood and stretched her neck. She sighed as it cracked when she twisted it.

"Hey, guys, I need a break. Do you mind if I step out and take a walk to the stables and visit Jezebel and Magnus?"

"Of course not. Do you want company?" Addison asked.

"*Non*. I just need to clear my head."

"Should we call it a night?" Sergei asked.

"I'm not ready to quit just yet, but I can't focus right now so I thought a walk would help."

"Okay. Then, holler if you need us. We'll come running," Sergei said.

"Please, we are perfectly safe here." Sophie laughed.

After pulling her jacket off the hook, she stepped out of her office and shut the door behind her. The silence that surrounded her in the barn was stifling. She stuffed her hands into her pockets and strode out the large door, her step determined as she sucked in the fresh, crisp air. Night had fallen, bringing a stillness with it that was relaxing. The crisp spring air filled her lungs and cleared the cobwebs from her head.

The horses were restless in their stalls. Their neighing and whinnying carried out to the pasture. There was something so distressing about the way it sounded that she picked up her pace and hurried toward the stables. The first thing that caught her attention was the darkness. The low blue night-lights came on like clockwork once the sun started to set. It had been that way since she was a child, but not tonight. *Strange. Why aren't the lights on?*

Shivers wracked her body as she paused at the entrance, the horses' distress evident by their stalking around in their stalls, but she couldn't see a thing in the pitch black. Fumbling at the wall just inside the doorway, she tried to remember where the light switch was, confused since it had been years since she'd had to use it.

Finding it, she flipped the lights on. The sudden onslaught of light blinded her momentarily. As she blinked to acclimate her sight, she glimpsed Jezebel moving around in her stall. Taking a step in Jezebel's direction, something struck her from behind. A sharp pain shot through her head. Her vision blurred and everything went dark.

CHAPTER 24

Facing Demons

Claude

Claude trailed behind his mother as she rushed into the stables. They had parked on the other side of their old house, not wanting to advertise their presence. He wasn't sure what kind of reception they would receive if they were to be seen here after hours, considering the way things were when they left. They should have waited until morning but, caught up in his mother's excitement, he hadn't considered the implications earlier. There was no one around, which gave off an ominous vibe considering the issue of the drugged horses. Then again, with the accusations focused on him, maybe there was no longer a concern about the safety of the animals, though it just didn't sit right with him either.

The lack of light bothered him. In all his years at the farm, he couldn't recall a time when the horses had been left alone in the dark. Eager to reach Jacques, his mother's pace far outstretched his. She was certain Jacques remained on-site once she'd spotted his car parked beside Paddock B.

Claude assumed Jacques had been put to work watching the farm at night, since he was still here long after most of the staff had gone home. The regular lights suddenly came on in the stables. The white light filled the area with blinding brightness, unlike the usual gentle blue lights that were left on overnight.

He lagged a good ten feet behind his mother as she turned the corner into the stables. Her voice pierced the air as she called out Sophie's name, making his blood run cold. Racing to catch up with her, he slammed into her where she stood, just inside the opening. The horses were agitated, their neighs nerve-wracking, and his mother chattered incoherently. Glancing over her shoulder, what he saw made his heart stop. His world turned upside down, and though there were shouts and other voices, his mind closed itself to everything and everyone around him. The only thing filling his vision was the crumpled form of

Sophie lying a few feet inside the stable door. Rushing to her, he dropped to his knees and immediately reached for her arm. His chest was ready to burst from holding his breath. Feeling her faint pulse he let out an audible hiss, clasping her hand in his.

She's alive. Oh, God. His eyes began to fill. He had never been so afraid in all his life.

Seconds later, Sergei and Addison rushed into the barn. Addison came to his side. "Claude, what happened? What's wrong with Sophie?" she cried.

Claude tore his eyes away from Sophie and looked up as Sergei stopped beside his mother and put a hand on her shoulder. She leaned into him as her body shook with barely-contained sobs.

"Call for help. She's hurt. I don't know what happened," Claude said.

Sergei nodded and stepped away to the phone on the stable wall near the light switch, when Claude's mother choked out, "Jacques."

Claude's head whipped back up as he stared at his mother. How could she be thinking about him right now while Sophie lay bleeding on the ground? "*Maman?*"

Leila's body continued to shake violently as she stared at her son. "It was Jacques."

"I don't understand."

"I saw him as I entered. Sophie was next to him on the ground and when I called her name he ran out the back door and threw that down," she whispered. She pointed to the corner of the stables near Jezebel's stall. On the ground, a large rock, covered in blood, leaned against the wall. She began crying in earnest. "I'm sorry. I trusted him. I didn't know. I am so sorry." Her voice hushed, her words came out in a jumbled mess.

Sergei returned to Claude's mother and wrapped his arm around her shoulder. "I've called the house. They're taking care of everything."

Claude squeezed Sophie's hand. His tongue stuck to the roof of his mouth, tangled in a sea of molasses. "Sophie, help is coming. Just hang on." The numbness in his chest trickled down to his legs. The whirlwind of voices surrounding him held little interest as his gaze never left Sophie's face.

Carson and Eddie came into the stables, breathless from their dash from the main house. "What is wrong with *Mademoiselle*?" Carson asked, stopping next to Leila.

"Miss Sophie?" Eddie kneeled next to Claude and took Sophie's other hand in his.

Marte came in just as the shrill of sirens sounded in the distance. "Help is on the way. Bertrand is coming."

"Good. Thank you, Marte," Addison said, her hand resting on Claude's shoulder.

The emergency crew arrived minutes later and immediately jumped into action. After checking her vitals and cleaning the wound on her head, they bandaged it up and bundled Sophie onto the stretcher. Claude stumbled to his feet as they lifted her up and began rolling her out of the stables. Claude had yet to release Sophie's hand.

"Can you tell us what happened?" one of the medical attendants asked Claude.

"We aren't sure. She was on the ground, unconscious, her head bleeding when we arrived. We believe she may have been struck by a rock."

"Struck by whom?"

Claude shrugged and pointed to the rock on the ground a few feet inside the doorway. He didn't doubt his mother for one moment. If she said it was Jacques, then it was the truth. But he was sure Bertrand would want to deal with him first.

"I see. Let's get her to the hospital."

Claude nodded, still grasping Sophie's hand as the EMTs continued pushing the stretcher toward the ambulance. Once they reached the back of the medical transport, he exhaled a loud rush of air. His hands fisted, hiding his trembling fingers. "I need to go with Sophie. She shouldn't be left alone."

"*Oui,* go with Sophie and your mother. There's nothing you can do here. We'll wait for Bertrand and then meet you there." Addison leaned in and kissed his cheek as Sergei led Leila to where Claude stood beside the stretcher. "I believe she's in shock. Can you take her to the hospital with you?"

The medic's hand paused on the door. "*Oui,* of course." He pushed the stretcher into the ambulance before taking Leila's hand and helping her into the seat beside it.

Without another word, Claude climbed up and sat down next to his mother on the long bench beside the stretcher Sophie was strapped to. His mother leaned into his side as his fingers closed around Sophie's sleeve. Resting his head against the steel wall of the ambulance, his stomach in knots, he closed his eyes, hoping to keep the nausea down.

CHAPTER 25

Making Amends

Sophie

S ophie opened her eyes to a blinding white light. *Heaven help me*. Unsure where she was she tried to take in the room, but it wouldn't stop spinning. She slammed her eyes shut so they couldn't pop out of their sockets. Her head throbbed like she'd lost a boxing match. And her entire body ached as though she'd been hit by a train. The voices surrounded her like a cloud, or a suffocating mist. She couldn't understand what anyone was saying, as they all spoke at once.

She dug through her befuddled mind, trying to remember. Her last thought was how dark the stables were, and fumbling for the light switch on the wall.

Jezebel had been whinnying in her stall and she was going to go to her when... That was all she remembered. Her eyes burned as if filled with shards of broken glass, so she stopped pushing.

"Please wake up." Bertrand gripped her hand and squeezed.

"Papa," she croaked. Her voice sounded far away and unlike her own.

"She's awake." Addison's voice came from somewhere on the other side of her. She opened her eyes again, only to be blinded as the pain increased.

"Lights hurt," she whispered.

The lights were turned off in the room, so only the illumination from beyond the door filtered in.

"Where am I?" she asked.

"Hospital—" the jumble of voices responded.

"Is she awake?" Leila asked from the lighted doorway.

"Yes, please come in," Bertrand said. Claude and Leila made their way into the room.

"Leila, how are you feeling?" Sergei asked.

"Fine. Just fine. A little shook up. How is Sophie?" Leila asked.

Sophie pushed herself up in the bed. "Claude?"

"I'm here." Claude stepped closer to the bed, into her line of sight so that she could see him.

Her father stood and leaned in, kissing her on the forehead. "We'll leave the two of you alone to talk." He clasped Claude on the shoulder before ushering everyone out of her room.

Claude sat down in the chair Bertrand had just vacated and took a deep breath. He looked miserable. Like a fish out of water as he sat there staring at her. She had never seen him so forlorn.

"How—" he said.

"Why—" Sophie paused and took a deep breath. "You first."

"How are you?" he asked.

"I think there might be a rabid troll in my head."

Claude snorted.

"Why were you at the farm?" she asked.

"*Maman* wanted to talk to Jacques. She thought he might be able to help prove my innocence."

"You don't need to prove anything to us."

"Of course I do."

She struggled to sit up.

He rushed to his feet and plumped the pillows as she pressed the button to lift the bed into a better position for sitting.

Taking his hand, she kissed the knuckles. "*Non*. We owe you an apology. I should have run after you that day. I wanted to but Papa said not to, to leave things alone. I am sorry I listened to him."

"How could you believe that of me?" he asked, pulling his hand from hers. His voice held a chill as he looked past her, avoiding looking her in the eye.

"You fool. We knew you didn't do it. How could you doubt us?"

"Then why?"

"I'm afraid Papa thought you and your mother were safer away from the farm. He was focused on flushing out the real culprit before someone really hurt the horses and one died, and we didn't want to see you dragged into it any further."

Claude's eyes grew wide as he stared at her again. "He used me, and you let him."

"*Non.*" Sophie's voice rose. "Jacques did. We just allowed him to think he succeeded in framing you." She took his hand between hers.

"How could you know this?" he muttered.

"Because we never lost faith in you. We never questioned your character. We did you a great disservice by not confiding in you, this I don't deny."

"*Oui,* it was tantamount to a betrayal."

"I didn't expect it to go on as long as it did. If you had bothered to answer any of my calls or my texts, you would have known days ago." She dropped his hand back on the bed and crossed her arms.

"I turned off my phone. I retrieved your voicemails only moments ago."

"Well, then, we share equal responsibility for this travesty continuing as it has. Wouldn't that be a fair assumption?"

"I should have called you."

"*Oui*. I was so worried. I didn't know where you had gone, or if you were safe. I hated that you were hurting. That you didn't know the truth."

"You didn't try very hard. If you had really wanted to find me, you could have."

"Claude, I called. I figured when you were ready to talk to me and hear me out, you would answer my calls, or at least listen to my messages."

"I didn't want to hear anything else. Knowing when it comes down to it you'll choose your father and your family name over me and us was more than enough," he ground out through clenched teeth.

"That's not fair. I didn't choose anyone or anything over you. *Oui,* I should have stopped my father that day. I should have made you stay. I was wrong. But don't you, for one minute, think I'd ever choose anything over you!" she shouted. She winced. Raising her voice only made her head pound harder.

Claude blanched.

She dropped her shoulders and untwisted her arms, reaching for his hand again. "Together, remember. We are in this together."

"*Oui.* I'm sorry I doubted you. What happens now?"

"We do what we set out do before. Find the truth."

"How?"

"Start at the beginning—"

The doctor walked in at that moment.

"And how is *Mademoiselle's* head?"

"If I say it's fine, can I go home?" Sophie asked through tight lips.

The doctor chuckled. "Let me take a quick look at you." The doctor flashed a silver penlight into her eyes. The white laser-like light pierced her pupils, making the room spin. She couldn't remember what she'd had to eat last, but she was certain it was going to make its presence known if the doctor didn't stick that light somewhere else. *Anywhere else.* She swallowed the lump in her throat and imagined herself in a cave. *A dark, quiet cave.* Bile churned in her stomach.

"You have a minor concussion, so I can only release you as long as you aren't going home alone," the doctor said.

She was pretty certain there were two doctors

staring down at her at the moment. Not that she'd ever admit she was seeing double. So, she aimed her gaze at the space between the two men standing over her bed.

"She won't be alone," Claude said.

"Okay, then, I'll sign the papers and you are free to go." The doctor scribbled something on his clipboard and, with a nod at Claude, left the room.

Recalling her conversation with Sergei and the stress and fears of the last few days, Sophie closed her eyes and took a deep breath. Opening them again, she searched Claude's face as she reached for his hand. Clasping it tightly, she steeled her nerves. "I need to tell you something. Something I should have told you years ago. But I was afraid to..."

"Afraid? To talk to me?"

She squeezed his hand. "Please let me get this out before I talk myself out of it."

"Fat chance of that now." Claude grinned at her.

"When I was in Russia, I was assaulted." Her eyes filled.

Claude sucked in his breath in an audible hiss.

"It's not as bad as you think," Sophie said in a rush of words. "I wasn't raped."

His shoulders tightened and lips flattened. "So you were mugged?"

"Not exactly."

"But you were not raped?" His words came out as a sound similar to the scraping of nails across a chalkboard.

"Not exactly."

A low growl escaped Claude as he glared back at her.

"I was at a club I shouldn't have been at. It was raided and I was separated from my friends. Alone in the back alley, three men came at me. They pinned me down and tore at my clothes."

Claude's hand gripped hers in a stranglehold as he closed his eyes and took a shaky breath.

"Others came to my rescue just in time." She sniffled.

"Where was Addison? Sergei?" he asked, his tone accusing.

"They weren't there."

"Why not?" His voice barely concealed the anger underneath.

"Claude, they didn't even know I'd gone. They studied. A lot. I well... I didn't," she said as embarrassment stained her cheeks.

"I see."

He clearly didn't by the stiff set of his shoulders and the lack of circulation in her hand where his held on for dear life.

"As soon as Addison came back to the dorm room and found me, she took charge. Both she and Sergei cleaned me up and took care of me after that. I never went to another club again."

"Why are you telling me now?" he asked.

"I thought it might help you understand my impatience to be married. My need to feel settled."

"Why didn't you tell me when you came home? I knew something was different. You had changed. You flinched often when I touched you at first. You used to have night terrors."

"I didn't want you to see me differently. As damaged goods, or as a victim. I didn't want to give you a reason to not love me anymore."

"That could never happen, Sophie. You are my light."

"I'm sorry." Tears streaked down her cheeks.

With gentle thumbs, Claude wiped them from her face.

They were interrupted as the nurse came in. "I have your release papers, *Mademoiselle*. Let's get you ready so you can go home."

Claude squeezed her hand and stood. Leaning down he kissed her lips before striding out of the room, leaving the nurse help her get out of bed and dressed.

CHAPTER 26

Full Circle

Sophie

S ophie sat on the side of the bed, watching her best friend pack up and clean up their numerous toys and such.

Shaking her head at the mess surrounding them, Addison said, "I can't believe how much more they have now. For Heaven's sake, Sophie, you've spoiled them."

"*Oui*. That is the job of the godmother, is it not?"

Addison dropped the toy she held into an open bag and laughed. "You, my friend, take things to the extreme."

"*Non*, this was tempered. I could have done so much more."

Addison groaned, making Sophie laugh.

"Agnes can finish this up while we take you to lunch. We only have another day together. Let us enjoy it. We have reservations at the *La Tour Eiffel* for this afternoon." She was satisfied with the awed look on Addison's face at the mention of lunch in the Eiffel Tower.

―――――――

Sophie strode off the lift at 58 Tour Eiffel and reached the large glass double doors first, pulling one open wide. Claude opened the second glass door and leaned his back against it as he ushered his mother in front of him and Addison followed, stepping through into the restaurant.

He winked at Sophie. "You know the man is supposed to do that."

"Hmm... Whatever." She grinned over at him.

"Serious. It's a gentleman's job." His tone held a note of mock severity. Sophie snorted in response.

Bertrand and Sergei, pushing the strollers, slipped through the open doors, laughing at their exchange.

As they passed, Sophie and Claude released their respective doors and brought up the rear. "Yes, that's true—it is very gentlemanly to hold a door open for a woman."

He bobbed his head so hard she thought it might fall off.

"But it's also just a human decency to hold the door open for people regardless of their sex."

"Touché." Claude whispered in her ear.

They caught up to their group at the maître d' station. The cheerful family atmosphere of the restaurant on the first level of the tower was exactly what they needed.

The hostess greeted them and led them to a large table against the windows, giving them a magnificent view over the Trocadéro, Palais de Chaillot, and the metal structure of the Eiffel Tower. The sunlight glinted against the windows, bouncing off water glasses and silverware, and shining lacquered tables.

Everyone's attitude was enthusiastic and lunch was a festive affair. Sophie had wanted her friends' last day with them to be relaxing and enjoyable. Considering all the drama they had witnessed during their visit, it had already been more than memorable.

The waiters brought a wide array of various French delicacies for the adults, setting them in the center of the table. Sophie was pleased with Addison's and Sergei's wide eyes as the mini feast was presented.

When the children's meals arrived in little metal picnic baskets Maxim immediately reached for the closest one, knocking over a glass of water as he swung the heavy container toward him. The blur of motion happened in an instant, leaving Sophie sitting in a puddle of ice-cold water as it dripped off the table and into her lap.

"Ugh." Sophie hopped up. She pulled a squealing Maxim out of his chair, still clutching his little metal basket. "I've got you, kiddo."

In a flurry of movement and energy, the staff cleaned up the mess and set everything right again. After she put him back down, lunch resumed without any further mishaps.

The waitress brought out a tray holding a half-dozen crystal flutes followed by three others who carried bottles of Champagne. Sophie was distracted and didn't immediately notice that Claude had risen from his seat to stand beside her. She glanced up at him. *What are we celebrating?* He smiled down at her unspoken question. Saying goodbye once again to her friends was bittersweet. Once again, Claude was trying to make it easier for her.

A hush descended across the table, then drifted throughout the restaurant. Startled by the sudden silence that surrounded them, Sophie looked down to where Claude had dropped to his knees. He pulled out a small, square black velvet box.

He opened the lid and rested his hand holding the box on her knee. "I'm sorry it took me so long to get here. To realize that you were already the best partner, best friend, and lover..." The heat rushed to his cheeks as he glanced over at her father. Bertrand's brow rose and a smirk crossed his lips, but he said nothing. Swallowing hard, he turned his attention back to Sophie.

"I kept waiting, delaying, hoping to prove myself worthy to you, of you, never accepting that in your eyes I already was."

Sophie stroked his cheek. "I tried..."

He placed a finger on her lips. "I don't want to wait any longer for you to be my wife," Claude said. "I realize now that I've been too afraid of change."

The world started spinning much faster as her breath caught in her throat. Unable to reconcile what she was seeing Sophie remained mute, her gaze fixed on the stunning ring he presented. A brilliant white, emerald-cut diamond rose high in the center of a rose gold and platinum band filled with a glittering array of diamond Xs and Os, nestled in the black foam. It was a unique pattern that clearly had been custom designed. It took her breath away and left her speechless.

"Are you sure?" Sophie choked. She had waited for

this moment for so long that now she could hardly believe it was real.

"Sophie," Claude growled. "Do not be *difficile*."

Everyone at the table laughed.

"That's a pretty tall order, Claude." Sergei chuckled.

Sophie narrowed her eyes and glared at Sergei before returning her full attention to Claude. Her heart raced in her chest, her pulse drumming in her ears. She could hardly focus her eyes, they were welling with tears.

"Will you marry me?" he asked again.

"*Oui,* I'll be your wife."

"Hallelujah," Bertrand said.

The entire restaurant clapped and cheered in the background as Claude reached for her trembling hand. He slipped the ring onto her finger before awkwardly getting to his feet and pulling her into his arms. He then kissed her like she'd never been kissed before, until her mind went blank and everyone around them faded away.

Falling into Place

EPILOGUE

Sophie

A few hours later, Sophie rested her head against the back of the couch as Agnes fussed over her. The children were upstairs while they held another council of war. It had been a week since Jacques had hit her on the head, bringing Claude back into the fold. And though the headaches were few and far between, when they struck it sucked the energy right out of her. The long day and emotional lunch had only added to the war going on inside her head.

Glancing down at the new engagement ring that sparkled on her finger, the butterflies in her stomach danced as she twisted the ring around to better admire its intricate design. The rose gold made the diamonds' brilliance dance in the light. Claude sat beside her, his hand on her knee.

Bertrand walked into the study and poured himself a drink before settling in his favorite chair. "I received another report from the investigator."

"What does it say, Papa? Is it really Jacques behind it all?"

Silence descended in a fog upon the room as everyone stopped talking at once and directed their attention to Bertrand.

Her father sipped his drink before setting it on the side table and opening the file in his lap. "It seems that Jacques has been a busy boy. For the last five years, he's been trying to get a foothold back into the jockey business."

"A jockey?" Sergei asked.

"He didn't talk about his past much," Leila said.

"Apparently, Jacques was a jockey long before he became a horse trainer. During a race the horse had a heart attack, dropping on the track. Jacques's hip was broken during the fall, and he was told he wouldn't ride again," Bertrand read from the report.

"That explains the limp he walks with sometimes," Sophie said.

"They say that a certain Sheikh Shahid bin al

Khalid from Saudi Arabia offered him a position if he could convince us to partner with them for a new line of horses."

"Do we know them?" Claude asked.

"I vaguely recall someone about a year or so ago coming to the farm and asking to breed their horses to ours. I told them we only breed with European horses, to limit our bloodlines, and they left. I didn't think much of it at the time."

"So, what are you saying? That Jacques has been drugging our yearlings to what, secretly artificially inseminate foreign horses?" Claude's tone held a tone of incredulity.

"*Merde,* with everything going on I forgot to mention Wanderlust!" Sophie cried.

"Who's Wanderlust?" Addison asked.

"*Monsieur* Martin called me last week, asking the same thing. Apparently, in the Dubai listing there was a horse claimed to be the offspring of our Balthazar and a horse from Brazil."

"Brazil!" Bertrand shouted.

"I don't understand—" Addison said.

Everyone began talking over each other again. The voices were now raised and heated.

Claude whistled to get everyone's attention. "We need to stay calm. We don't want to scare the little ones." He looked to the ceiling of the room.

"*Oui,* I lost my head," Bertrand said.

"So, where does this leave us?" Claude asked.

"The investigator delivered his report to the *Gendarmerie*. Now we wait for them to tell us the next move," Bertrand said.

"And the money in my account? What do we do with it?" Claude asked.

"Papa?"

Bertrand shrugged. "If the *Gendarmerie* doesn't confiscate it as evidence, I suggest we leave that up to you. Consider it a bonus for the hassle of everything we put you through."

Claude's eyes grew wide.

Sophie leaned into Claude and caressed the back of his head. He lowered his face as she tilted her head up and kissed his lips. Her heart swelled from the love within. She was happier than she ever thought possible. All was as it should be. Claude was home, they were engaged, their future certain.

I wanted to take a minute to thank you for taking the time to read **_Her Heart's Desire_**.

I hope you enjoyed **Sophie and Claude's** *story as*

*much as I enjoyed writing it. If you did, I would greatly appreciate you leaving a review on the review site of your choice. You can leave a review on Amazon by clicking here: **Amazon Review.***

Reviews are crucial for any author and a line or two about your experience can make a huge difference in helping other readers find this book.

Did you like this book? Then you'll **LOVE** the third story in the The Letting Love In series ***His Heart's Promise***.

Check out ***His Heart's Promise's*** blurb below.

She finally has her happy ending. Will one tragic day leave her arms endlessly empty or teach her the measure of love?

Sophie Compte has everything she ever wanted. Deep into the plans for her long-desired wedding to her childhood sweetheart, the impatient heiress knows her biggest concern should be dodging the unfortunate title of bridezilla. But with the "I do's" getting closer every day, each disagreement leaves her worried they're tempting fate by bickering over nothing.

Regaining her equilibrium once the vows are said, Sophie happily heads off to Bali for her honeymoon. But after a tsunami strikes the island, her worst fears become reality when her groom is swept out to sea.

Overwhelmed by loss, can she find the strength to imagine a different kind of forever?

His Heart's Promise is the darkly hopeful third book in the Letting Love In romantic women's fiction series. If you like endearing characters, tense scenes, and stories that tug at your heartstrings, then you'll adore Dawn Baca's emotional rollercoaster.

Read *His Heart's Promise* to savor each tender joy today!
Start reading ***His Heart's Promise*** now!

SNEAK PEEK
Prologue

The stifling fog rolled in. It blanketed everything, leaving no visible light—like walking through a tunnel, no beginning, no end. Soundless, solemn, devoid of emotion. Not a single sensory impression.

A cocoon of mist surrounded Sophie, swallowing her in suffocating silence. The sense of dread permeated her every cell, rendering her unable to move. A sharp chill clawed its way into her bones, slicing clear through to her heart, leaving an agony so overwhelming it stole her ability to utter a sound.

An intense sensation of falling consumed her. Her stomach pitched, and she lurched. She reached out for him, her hand trembling, desperate for her lover, but her fingers landed on cold, lonely sheets. Her heart froze as the reality sank in.

He was gone.

Lost to her forever.

Despair flooded her. Peace shattered, the shards rained down around her as she screamed his name.

"Shh. Sweetheart, it's okay. I'm right here," Claude said.

Whipping her head toward his voice, she blinked, bringing the pitch-black room into dim focus. "Oh, Claude!" she cried.

He reached out and wrapped his arms tight around

her as tears dripped down her cheeks and onto his bare chest.

Sweat trickled down her back, soaking into her silk nightgown and adding discomfort to the lingering fear. The inky darkness of the room reminded her too much of the smothering fog, setting her nerves even more on edge. Her head throbbed as she tried to wrap her mind around the dream.

The nightmare had come again. It swooped in, seizing her heaving lungs, and lodged her breath in her throat while her heartbeat pounded heavily in her ears. Gulping in air, she focused on breathing, trying to calm her queasy stomach.

She never knew where it came from. Some immeasurable, unconscious threat to her happiness brewed within. She couldn't put her finger on it, but deep down to her core, she knew without a doubt something was just not right.

Sophie clung to Claude as hot tears rolled down her cheek, soaking the hair next to her ear. Being held in his arms soothed her rattled soul. She so desperately wanted to chalk these horrid dreams up to pre-wedding jitters. She wasn't a particularly superstitious person, but there was just something about them which made it hard to do.

He caressed the back of her head, pulling away the hair matted to the side of her face. The gentle strokes lulled her into relaxing, and she sank further into him.

"Talk to me, *mon amour*. What has you so scared?" His hands caressed her arms, moving up and down, rubbing away the gooseflesh pebbling her skin.

Sophie gulped back the tears. "There are these dreams where I reach for you, and you're not there."

"But that is not unreasonable, we don't spend every night together." His tone was dismissive as he patted her back.

"*Non*..." She paused, taking a deep breath. It filled her sore lungs with needle-like pricks. "It's hard to explain, but I sense it's more than just that."

"Oh, Soph, you worry too much. It's the wedding. You have to take a break from it. All this stress is not healthy."

His unenthusiastic response stopped Sophie short. The words died on her lips. There was no point protesting. If she couldn't make sense of the doom brewing within, how could she make him understand?

Start reading ***His Heart's Promise*** now!

Do you like **_FREEBIE_** books?
Sign up for my newsletter and get
<u>His Heart's Burden</u> for Free!

To read my blog, get the latest news, future release dates, or to join my ARC team sign up for my newsletter at *www.DawnBaca.com.*

Also by Dawn Baca

LETTING LOVE IN — WOMEN'S ROMANTIC FICTION

- **His Heart's Burden — (*An Exclusive Prequel Story*)**

- **Her Guarded Heart —** (*books2read.com/HerGuardedHeart*)
- **Her Heart's Desire —** (*books2read.com/HerHeartsDesire)*
- **His Hearts Promise —** *(books2read.com/HisHeartsPromise)*
- **Her Heart's Wish —** *(Coming Winter 2024)*
- **Her Heart's Secret —** *(Spring 2025)*
- **Her Lonely Heart —** *(Winter 2025)*
- **His Forgotten Heart —** *(Winter 2025)*
- **Her Fighting Heart —** *(Winter 2026)*
- **His Racing Heart —** *(Winter 2026)*
- **Her Jaded Heart —** *(Winter 2026)*

IN ANTHOLOGIES — CONTEMPORARY ROMANCE

- **That One Summer —** Windswept Whispers
  Winter Wishes and Holiday Kisses —
  Merry and Bright *(Winter 2024)*

Acknowledgments

This book is the product of hours of dedicated support from everyone. Thank you for your willingness to read and re-read no matter how many times I needed it, and for giving me suggestions for improvement every step of the way.

To my amazing crit partners, your support is immeasurable. Arel, Becky, Bonnie, Elsa, Esti, Leilah, Kathleen, Kingsley, Maureen, Peri, Ray and Roxann.

To my wonderful editors Kim Huther and Amabel Daniels, you always bring the best to light. To the Best Page Forward for the fantastic back of the book, and the amazing graphic artists at 100 Covers for the beautiful cover.

Thank you to my personal cheerleaders, Sherry Franssen Breinig and Jennifer Sosh who continue to help me with beta reads and everything else under the sun. I could not do any of this without you.

About the Author

An insatiable reader of all genres since her childhood, Dawn is a globetrotter hungry to discover new places and experience unique adventures.

She can be found indulging in her husband's first love of summer camping in the mountains or luxuriating in the open seas while cruising to exotic destinations during the frigid winter months.

When she's not jet-setting she can be found in Central

Valley California with her family and their many rescue animals.

To read my blog, get the latest news, future release dates, or to join my ARC team sign up for my newsletter at *www.DawnBaca.com*.

- facebook.com/DawnMBaca
- x.com/BacaDawn
- youtube.com/DawnBaca
- pinterest.com/dawnmbaca
- instagram.com/dawnbaca
- amazon.com/author/dawnbaca
- bookbub.com/profile/dawn-baca
- goodreads.com/dawnbaca
- tiktok.com/@bacadawn

executed to present accurate, up to date, reliable, complete
information. No warranties of any kind are declared or implied.

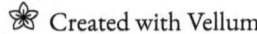